The King's Summons

ADAM GLENDON SIDWELL
&
ZACHARY JAMES

Super Dungeon Series
The King's Summons
The Forgotten King
The Glauerdoom Moor
The Dungeons of Arcadia
The Midnight Queen

Other Books by Adam Glendon Sidwell
Chum
Fetch

Evertaster Series
Evertaster
The Delicious City
The Buttersmiths' Gold

Other Books by Zachary James
Ama's Watch
"Reflexio"

The King's Summons

Published by Future House Publishing LLC under license from
Soda Pop Miniatures. All rights reserved. No part of this book
may be reproduced in any form or by any means without the
written permission of Future House Publishing at rights@
futurehousepublishing.com.
ISBN: 978-1-944452-84-1

Super Dungeon created by Chris Birkenhagen, John Cadice, and Deke
Stella
Series Story Development by Zachary James
Developmental editing by Emma Hoggan
Line Editing by Isabelle Tatum
Copy editing by Emma Snow
Proofreading by Alicia Davies
Interior design by Ahnasariah Larsen
Interior layout by Sarah Hagans

To my Buddy. As soon as I get done with work we can play toys.

—Adam

To my wife Kirsta, for believing in me like Princess Sapphire believed in Blaze.

—Zac

DIE MIDNIGHT TOWER

THE LORDSHIP DOWNS

VON·DRAKK MANOR

GLAURDOON MOOR

CRYSTALIA

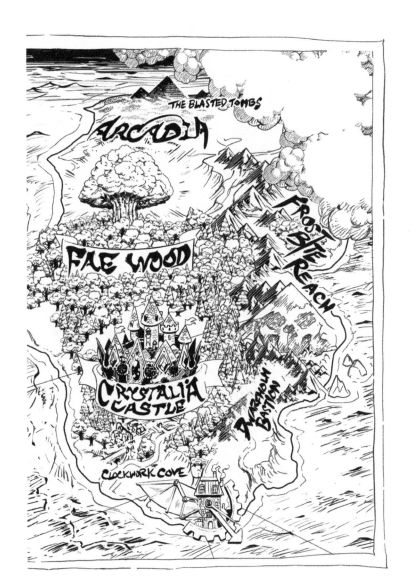

Foreword

This book, and even more so, The Super Dungeon Series, is the largest, most complex project we've taken on at Future House Publishing thus far. There are a lot of people who contributed their time, creativity, and brain power to get this series to press.

Here's where I get to say thank you.

But first, some backstory is in order. Here's how this series came to be: I discovered Super Dungeon tabletop games and miniatures on Kickstarter and fell in love with the art and the world. I emailed Deke Stella from Soda Pop Miniatures out of the blue nearly 3 years ago and suggested that we write books in the Super Dungeon Universe. To my delight, he agreed!

A cold trip to Boise, Idaho at Christmastime (where I stayed in a yurt) and a visit to the Soda Pop Miniatures and Ninja Division headquarters convinced me that Deke and the team were on to something. They were building worlds. We sealed the deal shortly after that.

Here are just some of the people that made this book possible: Zachary James, my coauthor and the series architect. He drafted the concepts and the spine for the whole series, which we eventually pitched to Deke. Zac did an incredible amount of research, and became Future House Publishing's Super Dungeon loremaster. He was also a confidant and friend while we struggled to get this off the ground.

I owe a great debt to the enormous contributions Dan Allen made to this manuscript. He also wrote book four. He's hilarious and we have whiled away many hours bouncing story concepts off each other. That's a rare thing to find in a friend. You should also see his family's Halloween costumes.

To Emma Hoggan, who had an enormous task on her hands, coordinating five books simultaneously, all while keeping the stories faithful to the Super Dungeon Universe. We authors, and perhaps most of all me, inadvertently gave her so much trouble over the years this series was in progress. Thanks for handling it with such incredible patience.

To Deke Stella and Chris Birkenhagen, who are the keepers of the world of Crystalia and the Super Dungeon Universe. After reading through the enormous notes they had generated, it was clear that Crystalia was an even richer world than the games indicated. We're so grateful to be allowed to play in such a magical kingdom.

Finally, thanks to you, the readers who have shown interest in my work, and who were willing to buy a book and take a chance. Thank you. Some of you have now become lifelong friends.

Which leads us to this story.

Adam Glendon Sidwell

Prologue

Hide-and-Seek

The halls of Crystalia Castle rang with laughter.

King Jasper III put down the map of his kingdom and listened as his giggling daughters ran past his throne room.

"She's got to be in the armor room!" Princess Citrine hollered from the front of the group.

A moment later, Princess Ruby gave a squeal of laughter. She had been found.

Only Amethyst, the youngest, was left.

Clever girl.

His daughters were too old for games like hide-and-seek—all in their teens or twenties. But once they all got together, there was no stopping the fun.

Princess Sapphire, the eldest and most serious of his daughters, and Citrine, his third daughter, already an accomplished warrior, had just returned from their inspection of the troops stationed in the Wandering Monk Mountains. Adventurous Emerald was back from the Fae Wood, with new stories to tell of the elves and the Deeproot Tree. And Ruby, ever a constant in Crystalian high society, had freed her schedule of admirers and negotiators.

Today was Amethyst's birthday. They would all celebrate together.

And soon, when the time was right, all of Crystalia would have something to celebrate.

The prophecy foretold it. Long ago, the Goddess bound her essence to the Dark Consul and drove him out of Crystalia. As she did so, she prophesied that five heroes of noble birth would rise up and defeat the Dark Consul once and for all and, by doing so, free the Goddess again from his clutches.

King Jasper III's daughters were the five princesses of prophecy: Princess Sapphire, Princess Emerald, Princess Citrine, Princess Ruby, and Princess Amethyst.

The king went back to his map and made notes on trade route attacks, attempting to triangulate possible locations of new spawning points, places where the Dark Consul's influence was creeping back into Crystalia from the Dark Realm.

A half hour passed. Jasper looked up. The voices were gone. The halls were quiet.

Where are they?

The king stood from his desk, walked swiftly to the window, and looked out over the garden yard that spread out between the tall castle and the siege wall. Ruby stood in the center of the yard, her hands cupped on her mouth, calling.

She turned and her face met his. Tears ran down her cheeks.

His office door banged open, and King Jasper whirled around.

Princess Sapphire stood in the doorway, buckling her sword belt and breathing heavily. "Have you seen Amethyst?"

"No. She was with the golem in the garden—surely you found her."

"Father." Princess Sapphire's eyes brimmed with tears. "We can't find her. And there's no sign of the golem either. Just Amethyst's footprints. Then they're gone."

"What?" asked King Jasper, dumbfounded. This couldn't be happening. Not here.

There was a horrifying screech of metal and a grinding of gears from the garden. Princess Sapphire turned and ran from the room. She drew her sword as she went.

Worry seized his heart. *No. Impossible.*

The castle warning bell began to ring. King Jasper threw open the window and leaned out, calling at the top of his lungs, "Amethyst!"

But no one answered.

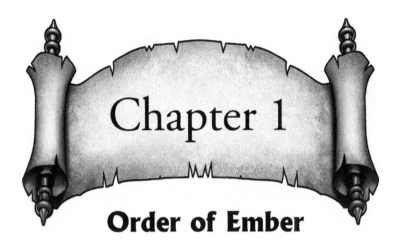

Chapter 1

Order of Ember

It had been two years since Princess Amethyst, child of prophecy, disappeared from her father's castle. Two years since anyone in all of Crystalia had seen her. Two years since the shadow of the Dark Consul had begun to creep ever closer and with greater boldness toward Crystalia Castle and the heart of the peaceful kingdom.

And now Princess Amethyst's father, King Jasper III, had even more dangerous problems at hand.

"My King," said the captain of the guard, "Our scouts

report spawning points a morning's journey to the east."

King Jasper III pulled the hood of his cloak lower over his face, despite the heat of the lava flows. Secrecy was critical to their mission's success. A king should never wander too close to the Dragonback Peaks, even *with* an elite royal guard. They were taking a terrible risk.

"And two more to the west."

"What type?" King Jasper asked.

"Rocktops. Even a few kobolds."

King Jasper considered this. He had not protected his kingdom by ignoring the threat of monsters. And they seemed to be growing ever more frequent since Princess Amethyst had gone. "They won't reach us in time."

He struck his sword downward into a lava flow at his feet and twisted the sword's hilt. The jewel on its pommel glowed blue. "We're here."

The lava parted and the rock underneath it trembled, grinding together as the earth opened its jaws. There was a staircase inside. The loremasters had been correct.

"Come," said King Jasper. He stepped down into the darkness. "We will trade one peril for another."

The captain of the guard stared into the shaft. There was worry in his eyes. "Sire?"

"This is why we came," said King Jasper. "Be at the ready. Bring all the men below. Guard our rear. Our mission lies underground." With that, King Jasper drew back his hood and descended into darkness.

The Kings Summons

The further he climbed downward, the hotter the air blew against his face and beard. The stone baked beneath his boots for sixty-seven steps, until finally he stood in a narrow tunnel lit faint orange by tiny threads of lava flowing down its walls.

Surely no king would come so close to the dragon Starfire's flaming realm were he not in great need. King Jasper felt the pain of his loss twist at his heart. His daughter Amethyst was gone. And now, in the last few weeks, things had gotten far worse.

He held back his tears. In this moment, there was no time for a father's sorrow. The two dozen guards behind him needed him to be a king.

They had followed him down the stairs, and now he led them into the passageway, their armor and swords clinking as they picked their way carefully along the broken ground. The hall opened into a wide, circular cavern. It was cast in a faint orange glow.

"Stop," he said, the sweat beading up upon his brow. Something wasn't right.

With a roar, a wall of flame erupted from the ground at his feet and shot toward the ceiling. It curved outward along the cavern's circumference forming a cylinder of flame. It held, surging upward in sheets, heat pouring from it onto King Jasper's skin, his cloak, and surely onto his guards' metal chest plates.

He heard them step back. One of them winced. But

not one uttered a cry of complaint.

Then a clear voice pierced the wall of flame. "Who dares enter the stronghold of the Order of Ember?" it said.

King Jasper stepped forward, despite the heat. "Wise Ember Mages, you know it is I, King Jasper the Third, defender of the Kingdom of Crystalia."

For a moment, it was silent. The wall of fire stuttered, then faded, and a circular, steaming crack in the ground was left in its place. King Jasper stepped over the gap.

The captain of the guard and his men followed close behind.

A second wall of flame burst from the ground in front of the king's feet. It roared to the ceiling above. King Jasper halted just soon enough, the heat pounding his face in waves. The first wall of flame erupted again behind him. He turned, shielding his eyes. They were trapped between two walls of fire, and more than a dozen of his guards were cut off from coming to his aid. The heat cut through the folds of his cloak.

Maintain your composure, he thought. *They're trying to intimidate you.*

The voice spoke again. This time King Jasper pinpointed the source: it came from within the center of the circle of fire.

"We know you, King Jasper the Third. And what is it that you seek?" it asked.

"A Hero," said King Jasper.

The Kings Summons

The wall of flame in front of him sputtered out and died. The one at his back did not.

He stepped forward.

A third wall of fire erupted from the ground at his feet.

The wall of fire behind him ignited again, cutting him off from all but the captain of the guard.

So this is how it would go. They were testing him. They wanted him deep within their molten grasp.

"Orders, Sire?" said the captain, his hand gripped tightly around his sword hilt. Sweat poured down his face.

King Jasper held up a calming hand.

The voice spoke a third time. "Many seek a Hero in the Order of Ember Mages. For what purpose do you seek yours?"

"For my daughters, who are lost," he said.

The flame sputtered, as if wavering.

"Daughters?" said the voice. As clear and strong as it was, it sounded confused.

King Jasper bowed his head. "Daughters."

The wall of fire in front of him died out. He stepped over the steaming crack that was left in its place.

His captain moved to follow. King Jasper waved him back. "From here, I go alone," he said, and the wall of flame behind him shot upward, cutting him off from his last guard.

King Jasper faced the center of the circle. Twelve columns of flame burst from the ground, flickering until they died away. Twelve mages in shining red cloaks stood in their places. Each held a curved wooden staff with a burning gem at the center of its crook. Each had eyes that burned with a yellow flame. The council of the Dragonback Order of Ember Mages.

"Your honesty has granted you an audience," said a tall woman at the center of the line—the Archmage. It had been her voice that spoke through the fire. Now it came from her lips.

The Dragonback Order of Ember Mages was as dangerous as it was unpredictable. A rogue order, they considered themselves superior to other Ember Mages, but they held great power. They were King Jasper's best hope. Even his loyal mages at the Tower of Ember in Castletown had told him this was his best chance.

King Jasper knelt on one knee. As a king, he bowed to no one. As a diplomat, he made exceptions. He needed their help. "Your Excellencies, you know that my last born, Princess Amethyst, went missing two years ago. You know the danger that poses to the kingdom—and even the seat of your council, especially as close as it is to the dragon Starfire."

The tall woman's eyes burned a faint yellow. "Yes," said the Archmage. The rest of the twelve nodded and whispered to one another. "And who in all of Crystalia does not know the Prophecy of the Five?"

All twelve of the council members spoke in unison:

The Kings Summons

Be at peace my children, but do not fall into idleness.
Darkness will return; it is a part of this world as much
as I.
Do not despair, for valiant hearts will once again return
it to shadow.
When I am needed, you will find me in five souls of royal
blood.
United, they will once again cast away the darkness.

Then silence hung in the air.

The Archmage spoke. "When the five unite, so shall the Goddess return and the Dark Consul's power break forever.

"And we know that your daughters must survive to fulfill the prophecy. The servants of the Dark Consul venture ever closer. They grow in strength and numbers. The time for the final battle with the enemy approaches."

King Jasper bowed his head. He needed to show them reverence and play by their customs. This is what they'd expect. He needed them now.

"And now all *five* of my daughters have gone missing," he said.

The twelve council members erupted in a flurry of conversation with one another. They hissed under cloaked hoods, their voices more like crackling flame than words.

"Quench your fury," said the Archmage. She rapped

her staff on the stone. They went silent at once.

"All five are gone? How could this be?" she asked.

"They are full of courage, and love for their youngest sister," King Jasper replied. "So they have each departed to seek her in the many realms. My eldest, Princess Sapphire, heir to the throne, left six weeks ago. She has not returned. Nor have we heard word from her."

It felt like he'd dumped a weight of stones from his chest. There. He'd said it. He'd shown how vulnerable he was. He was in their hands now.

The woman considered this. "And so you seek a Hero from our ranks to find what you have lost."

"A Hero, strong in body and powerful in magic," King Jasper said.

"It is a difficult thing Your Highness asks of us," said the Archmage. "Our Ember Mages are already deployed fighting the scourge of spawning points. And we of the council are too aged for such a long and dangerous journey."

"I make a royal request." King Jasper stood. "Upon your honor as Crystalians."

The Ember Mages erupted in conversation again. They spoke furiously back and forth to one another. Their debate lasted longer this time. And the minutes stretched on. This time King Jasper caught a few of the words. Hero. Rejected. Staff. Broken. Eyes of crimson. Then a mage with a braided beard cried out, "He wants a mage—

give him one. You know of whom I speak."

The circle of fire crackled all around them.

"We can't. Not *her*," cried another.

"She has promise . . ." said a thin man, his eyes bulging, "And prophecy is at stake . . ."

There was more arguing.

Finally, the Archmage rapped her staff once more on the stones. They were silent.

"The king has spoken! So it shall be granted."

King Jasper bowed his head.

"Though I warn you, your Hero may not be what you expect," said the Archmage.

The eyes of the council stole glances back and forth at each other. Was that guilt in their faces? Or uncertainty?

"Not what I expect?" asked King Jasper. They were hiding something. They all were.

"We say no more. You shall have your Hero. May she complete her quest and may the Prophecy of the Five be fulfilled. Goddess protect you and hold back the darkness."

Chapter 2

Crystalia Castle

The summons smoldered in Blaze's burning hands. It was the king's fault. What else could she have done? Blaze was an Ember Mage, the most powerful wielder of fire and brimstone in all of Crystalia, and she came and went as *she* pleased.

Now the king was forcing her, by royal summons, to his castle.

Of course she had lost her temper! Of course her hands had smoldered with rage, burning away more than half the parchment until the scrawling script of King Jasper III's hand was no longer legible. Even his official wax seal had melted into a blue smear.

Better to send messages etched in stone to an Ember Mage.

At least Blaze had read most of it before it had burned away. "By royal decree, I, King Jasper the Third, summon you to my throne in the inner keep of Crystalia Castle before the sun sets in two days' time." That had been the most important part, right? The rest was just details.

The messenger had found her on the edge of the Fae Wood two days ago.

So, Blaze had made her way, however reluctantly, to the sprawling city which was Castletown. It was a sight to see, with its shining white walls and towering blue minarets.

If she was honest with herself, she *was* curious. What did the king want with her?

Did he know about her being expelled—her *leaving* the Order of Ember by choice? She hadn't meant to burn that apprentice so badly. They were sparring. Blaze's fire got out of control. That had been an accident.

It wasn't my fault. It wasn't my fault.

And now they'd taken away her staff. What good was an Ember Mage without a staff?

But none of that was the king's business, was it? She might have to talk her way out of this one.

She picked her way through the winding streets of Castletown, her face hidden beneath her blue hood.

Crystalia Castle was more than just a castle now. It had grown into a sprawling city over the years, the kings building concentric walls of protection to accommodate the steady flow of races and cultures that sought refuge there. There were dangers in the lands outside Crystalia Castle's walls. Blaze knew all too well of the monsters one could find in the woods.

"Dwarven horns! Silk gloves! All at a very good price!" called the merchants from their carts. Towers reached skyward above the streets, their blue spires seemed almost to pierce the clouds.

A bent old woman sidled up to Blaze and whispered in her ear, "I've got some lemon crystals, or fizzy potions! Take your pick. Maybe some bottled sand from the Blasted Tombs?"

Blaze ignored her. Blaze had no time for alchemists today. Such strange things they sold here. Perhaps some adventurers would consider them good luck charms. She couldn't see the point. Blaze didn't need luck. Not with her powers.

Blaze skirted a pack of gnomes who were muttering back and forth to each other over a scaffolding they were building in the middle of the street, their pointed hats all aimed to the center of their huddle, their beards covering their squat bodies, tools and explosives clanking and dangling from their belts, their goggles pulled down over their eyes.

"It won't send that much shrapnel—just light it off," cried one of the high-pitched voices.

Blaze picked up her pace.

A lone freyjan brushed past Blaze's shoulder, her feline tail curling out from beneath her cloak, her furry ears twitching this way and that. She hissed at the gnomes. Deep bass dwarf songs bellowed out from the taverns. An elf bumped her shoulder as he rushed past. There were just too many people here. Like they were pressing in on her from all sides. It set Blaze on edge.

And when she was on edge, she could feel the heat begin to rise from her back up toward her neck. Too much heat turned to flames. *Calm*, she told herself. *You've got to keep it together.* She couldn't afford another mistake—not here.

Then she was at the edge of the castle drawbridge at the center of the city. It was lowered over the moat. Crystalia Castle's blue banners whipped in the wind high above her.

"Halt!" cried one of the five guards blocking the entrance to the keep. They were all clad in gleaming armor, with blue sapphires embedded in their chests, helmets pulled low over their eyes, the sunlight glinting off their polished iron spears.

Typical. They would be a majestic sight, were they not standing next to an Ember Mage such as herself. Her combat power far outmatched theirs. But it needn't come to that. She held up the summons. Or what was left of it.

"Hello, handsome fellas. The king has requested my presence," she announced. She couldn't help but add a hint of superiority to her voice. It felt so good to say that.

The lead guard raised the visor on his helm. He focused his eyes on the singed scrap. "By this pitiful shred of parchment?"

The four guards at his flanks broke into laughter.

"He did not tell you of his summons?" asked Blaze. A thin wisp of smoke rose from the scrap and curled into the air, as if betraying her. She could feel her neck heat up again. Her anger started to fuel the fire within.

"No, rogue. Nor would we believe it if you held it in your hand," said the lead guard.

"A summons by King Jasper the Third to Blaze, an Ember Mage," she started to read. At least *that* part was still intact.

"An Ember Mage?" called one of the guards. "Then where is your staff?" At this, the guards bellowed in laughter, slapping each other on their backs.

That stung. It stung so deep that the spark within Blaze caught, and the fire inside began to smolder red-hot. Good. *Feed the anger.*

The lead guard turned serious. "I don't know who you are, or what you're playing at, but there have been enough imposters in our midst as of late."

The Kings Summons

The four guards lowered their spears at Blaze.

"Be gone from here," said the lead guard. They advanced in unison, taking a single step toward her.

Blaze threw back the hood of her cloak. "I think not," she said. Her hands were glowing hot. Suddenly, she *really, really* wanted to see the king.

The guards rushed her all at once, charging over the dozen yards across the drawbridge between her and them, their long iron spears pointed at her heart.

The audacity! She, being summoned here to see the king, and given this reception? The fire within flowed out from her chest and into her fingertips. Her hands glowed. The guards would pay.

She threw out her hands, flinging brimstone toward the guards, flames shooting from her fingertips. The brimstone slammed two guards full in the chest, knocking them backward. The other three skidded in their tracks.

"She *is* an Ember Mage!" shouted one.

"That's what I said!" shouted Blaze. These guards were so frustrating!

The other two guards flanked her from behind, their lowered spears cutting off her escape. Two more guards with spears rushed from out of the gate. Then another pair appeared atop the castle walls. They lifted crossbows and hastily cranked the hoist mechanisms to load the deadly steel bolts into place. That would be a problem. Ember Mages controlled fire, but they couldn't dodge crossbow bolts.

In unison, the guards at her sides thrust their spears toward her. She stepped in past the sharpened tips and caught the shafts in either hand. She held them there.

"Her . . . eyes!" called the guard on her right. His face went white with fear.

So it was happening now, just like it always did when her power peaked. Her eyes glowed red.

Fire erupted from Blaze's hands like a forge as she poured her heat into the metal. In less than a second, the iron shafts were glowing red hot.

The guards with the crossbows took aim.

Blaze squeezed handfuls of molten iron from the center of the poles, cutting the weapons in half. She spun, hurling the smoldering iron at the crossbowmen. One dodged, only to lose his footing and tip from the drawbridge into the moat. The other was struck in his chest plate, the lava melting through and igniting his clothing underneath.

The lead guard rushed Blaze, desperately stabbing his spear at her chest. She sidestepped, and pulling a large marshmallow from her pouch, slid it onto the tip of the guard's spear.

"You're going to need that," she said, smiling. The guard's mouth dropped open as Blaze shot a column of flame from her left hand, roasting the marshmallow to a crisp and wilting his spear like a wildflower.

"Oh sorry. You wanted golden brown?"

The Kings Summons

"Surrender?" said the guard weakly.

"How about golden black!" she said, blasting a fireball at the lead guard. He fell over backward, his armor smoking.

The other two shuffled two steps back. "Ember Mage! Ember Mage!" cried one. He was shaking. "Call for the king's Tabbybrook!"

Blaze froze for a moment. She'd heard of Tabbybrook Mages before. But where?

One window in a line of a dozen small windows on the face of the castle's keep swung open. With a hiss, a catlike freyjan—much like the one she'd seen in town—leapt onto the window sill. She looked like a furry human, with a catlike face, claws, and even whiskers. She held a wooden staff with a glowing blue orb fixed to its end. A single brass bell fixed to the end of her tail tinkled as she twitched her tail.

"Meow," she said carefully, narrowing her eyes at Blaze. Then she tossed her staff into the air and leapt down onto the drawbridge, landing nimbly on all fours. She caught the staff easily behind her head without so much as a glance.

"A cat?" asked Blaze. She smirked. "You send a kitty cat to fight *me*?"

Blaze formed a fireball in each hand. Making fire drained her—it could feel like she'd walked for a full day without food after a fight. And without a staff of her own to store her fire in, she had to summon it all from inside her. It put her at a disadvantage.

No matter. This would be over soon. She still had enough flame left before she'd have to recharge the fire within. She flung both fireballs at the Tabbybrook.

They smashed into the castle wall and dissipated as the Tabbybrook leapt over them, her cloak flapping in the wind.

Oh. This was bad.

The Tabbybrook extended her staff toward the moat. The blue orb glowed, and a purr welled up inside her until it grew into a deafening roar.

Blaze didn't like the look of this. She dug deep and mustered another fireball. This one flickered in her hand. She was running out of heat.

A jet of green, putrid water curled up out of the moat and smashed into Blaze, hitting her with the full force of a charging bull. It burned as it slammed into her chest, blasting her backward like a rag doll, her limbs wrenched at their sockets.

She hit the ground hard, the cobblestones scraping across her back.

She looked up as another jet of moat water smashed into her face. She choked on green liquid. It tasted like dwarf socks. Sputtering, she tried to rise as another jet of water shot toward her.

She managed to roll out of the way, when a fourth jet of water smashed into her from the side. She hadn't even seen it coming. Now she remembered—Tabbybrook Mages controlled the elements. This one could harness water, whatever its form.

Blaze was out of her element here. She had to *think*.

The Tabbybrook landed lightly in front of Blaze, its little brass bell tinkling as she twitched her tail behind her. "Meow," purred the Tabbybrook. She looked down at Blaze with such self-importance. This was humiliating.

The Tabbybrook raised both arms, her staff glowing as two columns of water rose up from the moat and converged in an arch over Blaze's head. The Tabbybrook smiled sweetly, baring her little white fangs.

Blaze tried to form one last fireball, but it poofed into nothing in her hand. She was *Blaze*. How could she be bested so easily?

But she was so tired, her bones were starting to ache with a dull chill. She barely had enough heat left to roast a sausage.

A thought struck her. Maybe she wouldn't need any more than that.

The arch of moat water formed into a giant fist above the Tabbybrook. The king's mage closed her eyes in concentration. Were that fist to smash down, it would extinguish any spark Blaze had left.

Blaze reached out, forcing everything she had left on a single point a mere arm's length away . . . the little brass bell on the Tabbybrook's tail.

The Tabbybrook's eyes flew open. She howled painfully and shot into the air.

The fist of water broke, splashing down on the Tabbybrook until she was soaked through, her ears sagging and her whiskers trembling.

Blaze poured her last spark into the bell. The metal sizzled as it burned the water away into nothing.

The Tabbybrook leapt into the air once more, howling and swatting at her tail, darting back and forth across the drawbridge until she finally leapt into the moat, screaming.

Blaze heard a loud and satisfying sploosh. She tried to chuckle, but she had nothing left.

The two remaining guards closed in on her, their swords drawn.

This was it then. It was all over.

Suddenly the portcullis flung upward, and an old white beard with a man behind it dressed in stately purple robes stepped out onto the drawbridge. He was flanked by more guards.

"Stop!" he cried. It was King Jasper III. His Royal Highness himself. He chuckled, his belly rumbling under his enormous white beard. "I suppose you didn't read my summons, did you? The part about using the secret side entrance so that no one would know you'd come?" Was that a twinkle in his eye?

Blaze was too tired to shake her head.

"Our meeting here was *supposed* to be a secret," said

King Jasper.

"What shall we do with her?" asked one of the remaining guards.

King Jasper waved the guards back. "Let her alone," he said. "She's about to embark on a very dangerous quest."

Chapter 3

Quest Revealed

The inside of Crystalia Castle's circular war room was exquisite, if not intimidating. The ceiling was a carefully fitted stonework dome high above their heads. Only a few shafts of light pierced the dim room through drawn curtains.

"A quest?" asked Blaze. At least she wasn't in trouble.

"Of the most dangerous kind," said King Jasper, his eyes fixed on Blaze as he said it. He had locked the doors and sent the guards away so they could speak in secret.

The Kings Summons

He leaned over a diorama of the hills, valleys, and cities of Crystalia. They were displayed in shockingly accurate detail, with scale models of every major landmass and landmark set in their rightful places. There were the Arcadian Dunes to the north, the Clockwork Cove in the south, and the Glauerdoom Moor to the west. Even the Midnight Tower's obsidian spires rose from the center of the model. Blaze couldn't help but feel a sense of foreboding at the sight of the Tower.

"And so you need an Ember Mage," Blaze said. Of course he did.

"Not just any Ember Mage," said King Jasper. "I went to great lengths to find just the right one."

"Then I accept!" cried Blaze.

King Jasper smiled. "And yet, perhaps I made the wrong choice, if my Tabbybrook defeated you," he said.

Blaze stiffened. She smelled like brimstone, though her body ached with a bone-numbing chill. It would be hours before she could get her spark back. And she had no staff to store her fire in. King Jasper looked her up and down. Did he know what disadvantage an Ember Mage was without a staff?

"Your Majesty, need I remind you who fell screaming into the moat?"

King Jasper chuckled. "I suppose so. I suppose so."

"There will be orcs," said the king.

Blaze narrowed her eyes. Rage smoldered inside her at

the very mention of orcs. Oh, how she hated orcs. "Then I accept! Bring them on," she said. She'd love a chance to fight them.

She looked over the landmarks on the map.

"And to where is this quest?" asked Blaze.

King Jasper stabbed a finger at a glistening ice mountain on the diorama. "The Frostbyte Reach," he said.

Blaze soured. "Then I decline!" She growled. An Ember Mage, in the freezing mountains of the Frostbyte Reach? Snow and ice and cold were not the way of an Ember Mage. The freezing temperatures would make it even harder to summon her fire.

King Jasper pulled a braided rope, and five sets of curtains opened all at once, flooding the room with light. Sunbeams shone through five beautiful stained glass windows encircling the room, each depicting one of King Jasper's daughters: Princesses Sapphire, Emerald, Citrine, Ruby, and of course, Amethyst.

"The Prophecy of the Five," whispered Blaze. She knew it by heart, just as most Crystalians did.

"And they are missing, every last one," said King Jasper. His eyes looked sad.

"Missing?"

"Why is everyone always so surprised when I say that?" asked King Jasper.

"Because you're their dad, right? They're not like the keys to the coach. How did you lose all *five*?"

The Kings Summons

King Jasper's face darkened. Blaze felt a stab of guilt. Maybe she had gone too far.

So she leaned over the map.

"Do you know what it's like to be alone in this world?" King Jasper asked her. He looked serious.

Blaze felt her heart twist. She thought of Midway, her home. It had been destroyed long ago. Her parents were gone. They had been for a long, long time. And the only family she had left—the Order of Ember—had banished her. "Yes," she said, almost in a whisper. She was staring at the place where Midway should have been on the king's map. She knew *all too well* what it was like to be alone.

"My eldest, Princess Sapphire, heir to the throne, is gone," said King Jasper.

Blaze's heart leapt at the mention of Princess Sapphire. She jumped to her feet. The spark, unbidden, lit in her chest. Memories flooded into her mind. Orcs. Midway. Burning.

"The enemy is moving in the Frostbyte Reach. Something is at play which I cannot discern—the distance is too great and the realm too vast for reliable communication," said King Jasper.

"Princess Sapphire—you allowed her to go?" said Blaze. Of course Princess Sapphire was gone. She was one of the five after all.

King Jasper nodded.

"And she hasn't—she's not . . ."

"No word," said the king. "In months." He turned and gripped the edge of a bookshelf laden with ancient tomes as thick as his fist.

"I'm sure . . ." Blaze began, but the words did not form on her lips. She wasn't sure of anything. The Frostbyte Reach was dangerous.

But Princess Sapphire? If anyone in all Crystalia could survive in the Reach, it was her.

Blaze had met her only once. That chance encounter had been enough to convince Blaze that there was no greater warrior in all the realm.

She blinked, focusing again on the king. "Why did you choose me?"

"This threat within the Frostbyte Reach, as yet unrevealed, might be my realm's undoing. I cannot fight two fronts—the Nether Elf hordes from the Midnight Tower on the one hand, and the orcs of the Frostbyte Reach on the other."

"But why me?"

King Jasper looked at her. He was studying her. "Why indeed?" he asked.

"I'm not . . ." Blaze began to say that she was no longer a member of the Order but couldn't force the words from her lips.

"I was told you were the one for the job," said the king.

That was curious. "Who would have said that?" she

asked. There wasn't anyone who believed in her. At least, they hadn't before.

The king looked solemn. "For now, let it be enough to know that I chose you."

Blaze looked down at her hands.

"Young one, I cannot change your past. But I need your help, nonetheless. I'm willing to offer three of my personal guards to—"

"I don't need their help," Blaze said quickly.

King Jasper smiled. "I admire your bravery. But understand, I have seen many things. War. Sorcery. Dragons. You must trust me, child. This task you cannot do alone."

"I'm not safe," Blaze said, through faltering lips. "I . . . I can't control the fire."

King Jasper took in a long breath. Blaze felt as though the Goddess herself were weighing her soul.

Just say something. She couldn't bear the silence.

At last he turned. Drawing a key from under his brightly embroidered tunic, he went to the fourth of five small jeweled boxes on a long shelf. He opened it and withdrew a glittering object.

Turning back to Blaze, he extended his hand and opened it. In his palm was a bright pink heart-shaped locket.

Blaze didn't know what to think. Of all the trinkets to offer her, this prissy bauble?

"Of this I am sure, former mage of the Order of Ember. You cannot succeed alone. So, I offer you this."

The locket was held on a woven, white lace necklace.

"I really couldn't," Blaze said, wincing.

"This amulet—"

"It belongs to Princess Ruby, doesn't it?" Blaze said. Princess Ruby, the king's fourth daughter, was the pretty princess of pink perfection herself. This object could only belong to her.

"Perhaps," the king admitted with a wry smile. "It is a powerful object, which you can open only when you are twice your strength." He held the lace necklace out with both hands.

Blaze didn't know what to say. This was not her style. But she couldn't refuse a gift from the king. Not here in his war room. She bowed her head, and King Jasper bestowed upon her the prissiest, most girlie jewelry she had ever seen in her life.

"Thank you." Blaze nearly choked on the words.

Princess Sapphire . . . Blaze clutched the locket, recalling the extraordinary events of the day she had met Princess Sapphire. *Does he know?* She ventured a question. "Sire, do you know where I'm from?"

The king just smiled, his eyes twinkling.

"Midway," said Blaze. She searched for a reaction in his face. She found none.

"I've heard of it," he said.

The Kings Summons

Of course he'd heard of it. He was the king.

Mere coincidence? To summon me to save her . . . after all this time. It was enough to make her wonder if another hand was involved. But that would be even more remarkable. Could the Goddess still be working her magic, weaving the tapestry of her creations—tying together those two threads that touched so long before?

"The Goddess has not abandoned us," King Jasper said, as he turned to a heavy wooden door at the back of the war room. He slid aside the heavy bar locking it and pushed the door open.

I hope he's right.

Blaze followed King Jasper down a winding staircase. He opened another heavy door. On the other side was a vast chamber lined by shimmering crystals the size of watermelons. A bent old magician stood behind one, beads of sweat clinging to his brow, his hands passing over the crystal until it conjured a bright sphere of light.

Travel by portal from the Castle was something Blaze had only ever heard rumors about. It was either very costly in magic to operate or very dangerous—or both.

The magician spoke a spell in a strange language Blaze did not recognize. The swirling sphere of light wrapped itself into a vortex of color until the center became as white as driven snow. And it probably was.

All sound in the room vanished. It was as though Blaze had simply been cut off from the rest of the Castle.

A quartermaster shoved a rucksack full of supplies into Blaze's hands.

"Go to the village of Hetsa. You will find allies there. I ask you, as your king—as a father—find my daughter," King Jasper said.

Blaze looked him in the eye. "I accept," she said quietly. This time she said it with resolve. She stepped through the glowing portal.

Suddenly, she was falling through space and time. Her stomach lurched within her. A burst of white and blue flashed around her, and Blaze found herself perched high on a cliff in a sheltered alcove lined by crystals just like those from the Castle's chamber. A path led upward, carved into the side of a steep cliff, surrounded by frozen waterfalls.

In a single heartbeat, she'd been transported to the Frostbyte Reach.

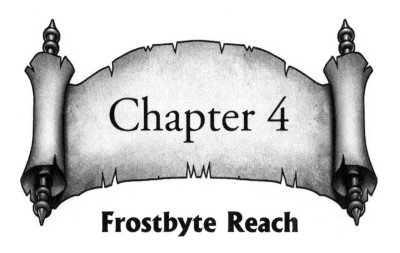

Chapter 4

Frostbyte Reach

It was ten years ago when Blaze saw her first orc.

Fire. Walls and ceiling ablaze. She was trapped. Her own screams echoed in her ears, frantically calling for help, only to be drowned out by the grunts and deep-throated war cries of the enormous creatures ransacking her village.

And then it all happened. The flaming door broke apart, and a girl all clad in armor rolled across the floor. She wore gauntlets and carried a sword and shield.

She could not have been more than ten years older than Blaze, maybe fifteen or sixteen years old. Her blue-gray armor shone in the flickering blaze set by the marauding orcs. "Come on!" the girl screamed, beckoning to her. "The roof is going to—"

The center beam broke, and the armored girl reflexively raised her shield. The roof beam slammed into the girl, driving her down to one knee.

"Climb under me!" she shouted.

Blaze could still feel the fear that had paralyzed her.

The girl sheathed her sword and shoved back a piece of burning wood with her gauntleted hand. "Got to . . . unggh," she strained.

Panic seized Blaze, and she reached out to help, pressing her own hands against the burning wood.

The girl's eyes widened in panic. She stared at Blaze's smoldering palm. Blaze drew back her hand. Had she done something wrong?

Then the girl laughed. "You have the spark!—listen to me. I'm going to get you out of here. I'm going to protect you."

"But the orcs—they . . ."

"Just come with me. You have a fire within," she grunted under the load of burning timbers. "Please. I promise to get you out of here. You have the spark. You must live so that someday you can become an Ember Mage. I am Princess Sapphire. I swear it will be done."

The Kings Summons

She sounded so certain, Blaze couldn't help but believe her. She crawled under the girl's legs and out into the street.

Princess Sapphire rolled clear of the rubble just as the rest of the house came tumbling down.

"You're safe . . ." Princess Sapphire started to say, when four huge orcs spotted them from farther up the road.

They charged.

Princess Sapphire thrust Blaze backward. "Run!"

The princess drew a second sword and dropped into a defensive stance. She had lost her shield in the burning house.

Was she really going to fight them? Four full-grown orcs? Blaze had never seen anything like it in her life.

It really *was* the Princess Sapphire; Blaze was sure of it. Everything about her—strength, courage, the way she moved, her armor, the glowing blue jewels.

But where were her guards?

Blaze should have run, but she stood rooted to the spot, coughing the smoke from her lungs as the great orcs, shoulders twice as wide as a man, heads the size of an ox's, raised their clubs and hammers and bellowed their war cries.

Their horrible faces burned into her memory. Each warrior bore a tattoo of a claw that wrapped around one eye—the infamous raiders of the Crook-Eye tribe.

The young princess stood her ground and bellowed

her own cry. "Come to me, beasts!"

The first orc raised its club and swung. Princess Sapphire hurdled the club, swiveling one leg above the other and twisting in midair. Her leaping roundhouse kick slammed directly into the charging orc's face, while its errant swing crashed into the second orc, knocking it through the burning wall of Blaze's home.

Blaze screamed as the third orc raised its great hammer and rained a crushing blow down on the princess.

But the princess's sword drew an edge of blue fire and sliced straight through the hammer's handle, while her other blade severed the suspenders holding up the orc's buckskin trousers. The raider tripped over its pants and fell on its face. Princess Sapphire's next swing came down on the fourth orc before it could raise its great sword. Her blow hit the orc's metal helmet like a hammer, and the helmet rang out like a bell. The tusked orc's eyes rolled back, and it fell like a sack of coal.

Blaze's jaw dropped. The teen princess had single handedly knocked out four orc warriors.

"Run!" Princess Sapphire commanded.

Blaze obeyed, retreating from the embattled village as two dozen royal cavaliers on horseback charged down the hill, the thunder of their horses' hooves drowning out all else.

The young Princess Sapphire, by riding ahead of her men, had saved Blaze's life. She had taken a huge risk.

The Kings Summons

And that had awoken Blaze's Ember spark. It was that day that she set on the path to become an Ember Mage.

And now Princess Sapphire was missing.

Blaze trekked through the snow of the Frostbyte Reach, wrapping her blue cloak tight around her.

First Princess Amethyst and now Princess Sapphire— how could a king lose a princess of prophecy? It wasn't like misplacing a shoe—the entire fate of Crystalia depended on all five princesses.

And why send a reject Ember Mage? Did the king really not have another Hero to send?

King Jasper was a seasoned tactician and, arguably, as great a master of lore as the long-lived elves. There had to be method to his madness.

Or was there? Could it be that his daughters' disappearances had brought on actual madness?

Blaze's inner fire had taken her to the halls of the Order of Ember. And when the fire had grown out of control, she had been cast out. She should have had a new family of mages to accept her. Instead, she had only shame, disappointment, and a firsthand knowledge of what she could not have.

And now she was walking alone in the mountains. All alone.

Blaze stopped on a ridge to catch her breath. If only travel by portal was more precise. They could have sent her straight to Hetsa. But they knew better than that.

Better to land at the crystal landing point than to risk getting dropped off the side of a cliff.

In the distance, she could barely see the last hint of the green plains that spread out from the base of the Frostbyte peaks.

These were the rolling, grassy hills and patches of shaded forest she had once called home.

Somewhere in those grassy hills, too far to see, was the tiny speck that was her home village of Midway—the exact midpoint on the road from Crystalia Castle to Yuyang. Beyond that were the Wandering Monk Mountains, rising in the distance, with the beautiful Path of 1,000 Shrines carved into their faces.

Not far from the village, a private cemetery with two headstones bore the names of her parents killed by Crook-Eye Orc raiders.

"Hello, Pa. Hello, Mum."

She spoke to them as though their graves lay before her. Somehow, the distance made it easier to find the words.

Blaze drew in a breath and held it before uncorking her bottled-up emotion. "I got kicked out of the Order—I was too angry. Too angry! Anger is what gives a mage their power. I don't understand. All I ever wanted was to stand up to the enemy—to fight the ones who took you from me. All I ever wanted was to send them back to the Dark Realm where they belong."

The Kings Summons

She shoved her hands into the oversized pockets of her travel cloak. "And now I'm going on a job that nobody else wanted—why else would King Jasper have asked me—and I'll probably die in the snow, and nobody will ever find me."

She pulled her blue cloak tight around her. It was the last tangible evidence of the Order she had once belonged to. It was all she had left. With a sigh, she trudged forward in the snow.

Her foot fell deeper than usual. She looked down, expecting to see a crevasse opening up in front of her.

It wasn't a crevasse. It was only a footprint.

A *large* footprint.

Not human.

Her palms tingled with sweat as her stomach twisted into a knot of anxiety.

How long had it been since she had seen one—ten years?

An orc.

Blaze carefully lifted her foot and stepped forward. There was another footprint in front of the first. It was a long stride, but not as long as she had expected. She took another step. Large feet, but medium pace for an orc—so it was growing but not full-grown.

This was an adolescent orc.

Blaze's palms tingled with a mixture of fear and excitement.

A scout perhaps?

Blaze itched to ignite the spark. She felt her temper rising into rage. Did she really dare fight an orc alone? If she saw one, she was almost certain it would come to that. She would *have* to defend herself.

But there was no guarantee how far away the lone orc was. She didn't want to flame out before reaching her quarry.

Blaze hurried ahead, following the footsteps down a set of switchbacks and charging around a large outcropping.

The slope shallowed into a bowl where the pines dotting the landscape grew low and dense. The footsteps in the snow continued into a tight grove.

She would either have to scale a steep escarpment on the rock face or go lower on the slope where a snow slide would put her far down the hill and away from her quarry.

Blaze lugged her pack across the bowl, heading directly for the copse of pines.

As she stepped between the trees, she found that several of the trunks shared a common base, like fingers growing from a hand. Other trunks had grown sideways and even buried themselves in the ground, as if twisted by some unseen force. There was no snow here, which was strange given the shade. The rocks underfoot were riddled with a shaggy moss and crumbled under her feet.

Something was wrong about this place.

Then she saw the skull.

The Kings Summons

The enormous white bone skull sat directly in her path. Trees curled over it from both sides in an ominous arch. The skull bore long fangs—too large for an orc.

Perhaps a gnoll? The skull was large enough to engulf her entire head if she were to stick her neck in it.

That was not going to happen.

The ground around the skull was littered with what looked like fragments of fine parchment. As she stepped forward, she noticed the pattern of scales.

Not parchment. Skin shed from some very large reptile.

Oh no.

She turned to charge back up the ridge. Just as she shifted her weight, the skull hissed, exhaling a noxious, black fog.

The fog swirled around Blaze, then glistened and began to coalesce at three points equidistant from the skull.

She had almost certainly discovered a spawning point. As scared as she was, Blaze was rooted to the spot. She couldn't look away. She was actually witnessing the emergence of life into Crystalia from beyond. Few experienced it.

Fewer lived to tell about it.

She knew from her lore lessons that the black fog that swirled from the spawning point was a mutagen. It carried the will of the dark demons, mingled it with the Goddess's vitality, and brought the three hallmarks of the

Dark Consul's influence:

Corruption.

Evil.

Destruction.

Here, in the frozen north, the essence was sure to form into something suited to the cold, something—

Three lizard-like humanoid creatures, draped in icicles, with red-stained fangs agape, rose from the snow where the fog had coalesced, their long crocodilian tails lashing aggressively.

A vile white-skinned ice kobold flicked its forked tongue as it leveled a blade-tipped polearm in her direction.

Ice Pick Kobold. Blaze was not excited about the prospect of losing her head to this weapon of wholesale dismemberment.

Its companion lifted a sling with a snowball and began whirling it. Blaze nearly laughed, before the snowball in its sling began shedding razor-sharp crystals in a wide arc.

If that snowball hit her chest, it might just send a shower of spikes into her heart.

"There she is—just one Crystalian human," said the Ice Pick Kobold.

The Snowball Chucker cackled with laughter. "We shall feast on this trespasser."

A streak of pure rage rose within Blaze.

"This is our world. Ours!" she said. "You are the trespassers."

The Kings Summons

The third ice kobold rose up out from the snow. Gray blue armor tinged with ice crystals that sparkled in the sunlight. This was an elite Frostscale warrior. It banged a blue steel sword against the skull emblem on its shield and raked its tongue over its fangs. "Your world is passing as the day into night. The Midnight Queen will see to that."

"The who?" asked Blaze. She'd never heard that name before. It didn't sound good at all.

"Kill her!" the kobold cried.

She had to ignore the chill. She had to fight the exhaustion in her legs. Blaze's rage burned through the fog in her head and tapped into the heat deep within her. Her spark lit, and the world took on a red hue.

"An Ember Mage!" The ice kobold swiveled its head and gave a guttural cry that sounded like a broken wagon wheel squeaking. "Eeeeeeeeeewa!"

She thrust her right fist out, blasting a fireball into the Ice Pick Kobold. The fire hit it square in the chest, knocking it backward. Its polearm went spinning away into the snow.

She blasted four more fireballs in quick succession at the Snowball Chucker and the Frostscale warrior, blasting them both backward into the snow.

The Snowball Chucker hurled a glowing snowball at her. Blaze didn't want to find out what the cursed snowball would do when it hit her skin.

"Fireball!" she cried, hurling a fireball nearly half as

tall as she was straight at the Snowball Chucker.

The snowball vanished in a burst of flame. The Snowball Chucker fell easily, but the Frostscale warrior stayed on his feet, huddling behind his enormous shield which had taken the brunt of her attack.

"Fireball! Fireball! Fireball!" cried Blaze, blasting three quick bursts of molten heat at him. The first two hit his shield, throwing him off balance. She caught him in the head with the third, and he screamed, the snow and ice on his scaly skin hissing as it burned into steam.

"Yes!" cried Blaze. Maybe she would learn to love the Frostbyte Reach after all.

Clouds of black fog spilled out of the skull at the center of the spawning point, rolling and coalescing into ten more ice kobolds.

Ice dripped from their dragon-like snouts, and their human-like arms held even larger swords, or heavy ball and chains. Each one bore a spiked shield.

"Uh oh," said Blaze. It was hard to hide her disappointment.

These hulking warriors were Blockheads—not the smartest but certainly the largest. Blaze had seen sketches of them in her training long ago. She had studied their names. And now they had come for her.

Blaze slammed her fists together twice until the pain in her knuckles doubled the fire within.

Not today.

An ice kobold at the back of the pack with a headdress

dangling with shrunken skulls pointed its priest staff at her. Three ice spikes grew right out of its head.

"Human . . ." it hissed.

A Frozen Priest too? Blaze shuddered at the hideous sight. Its scaly hide was old and wrinkled, and its eyes shone with pure hatred.

"Foolish, girl. Your magic is no match for the power we bring from the Dark Realm." Its crackling voice was raspy, like the scratch and crunch of feet on dry leaves.

The Frozen Priest hissed a command, and all ten of the hideous, pale-skinned lizards hissed in unison as they fanned out around her.

She needed time. She'd shot out that first barrage of fireballs so quickly, and her inner fire was not yet the vortex of roiling power she would need to fight so many enemies. She needed time to stoke it.

She was going to need *a lot* of fire to take down ten of these monsters. She'd never summoned that much so quickly, especially in the cold. And this was not the place to be caught slow-footed.

Blaze pulled back her hands, ready to form a sheet of flame, when the Frozen Priest swung a twisted skull-tipped staff in a wide arc. Dark magic poured from it, conjuring a whipping, icy wind that blasted straight into Blaze, knocking her backward and flinging her rucksack from her back.

Blaze picked herself up. Her rucksack lay open in front

of her, its contents scattered in the snow.

To her delight, a small, round flask with blue liquid inside sat inches from her nose.

"Fire Water!" she cried. She snatched the flask of blue liquid, uncorked the bubbling potion, and drank it in one gulp. She'd trained with Fire Water before. The familiar aftertaste of the Fire Water tingled on her tongue.

Less than a second later, Blaze's arms rippled with new heat. The snow melted around her, and ice crystals swirling in the air melted before they even touched her skin.

These potions really work!

And just in time too. She could hear the Blockheads beating their swords against their shields behind her as they charged.

She'd have to target one at a time.

No, she had two hands.

"Ahhhh!" cried Blaze, leaping to her feet, the inner fire swirling within, a torrent of power rising up within her. Her hands burst into flame. The Blockhead Kobolds hesitated. Fire was not their favorite. Well—there was plenty to go around.

"Fire Blast!" she cried, thrusting both hands forward at an angle and spreading them outward. The fan of flame knocked three Kobolds down and sent two more screaming in terror.

The Frozen Priest raised its staff. "Cutting Wind!"

48

it cried. A blast of cold snow whirled around Blaze. Ice crystals lashed at her as the whirlwind grew tightly around her, nearly blocking her view of her attackers.

Through the haze of whirling ice, Blaze was just able to make out the shapes of the remaining Blockhead Kobolds as they closed in on her from either side.

If Blaze was going to survive this battle, she would have to be able to see her attackers.

Letting the magic surge within her to a dangerous level, Blaze lifted a large stone at her feet out of the snow. She poured every ounce of heat from the Fire Water potion inside her into it. The rock hovered between her hands as raw energy swirled into it, like a whirlpool of heat.

The stone melted into red-hot lava.

"Magma Strike!" Blaze thrust both fists forward, unleashing the magma like a stone from a catapult. The Frozen Priest disappeared over the snow bank in a burst of fire, and the ice storm stopped abruptly, leaving her enemies in clear view.

Their source of magic cut off, the Blockhead Kobolds stopped and exchanged looks, either worrying for their own fate, or trying to come up with a new plan. Perhaps now they would retreat.

"Surrender?" asked Blaze. She was hopeful.

One of them raised its sword. "Our master!" it cried in a dull, slow voice.

The rest of the Blockheads screamed savagely, beating

49

their shields.

"Destroy the human!" cried the one closest to her.

As a swarm, the entire mass of Blockheads surged forward. In less than three paces they would all be on top of her.

Blaze tapped her anger, opening it to full and unleashing a rapid-fire barrage. "Fireball! Fireball! Fireball!" Three balls of superheated plasma found their targets, but now the Blockheads were in range with their own weapons.

Blaze unleashed a flash of heat to blind their eyes momentarily. She spun in a melee attack, sweeping the legs from under the largest Blockhead while blasting a double-handed fireball into the face of the next nearest attacker. She spun, releasing two fire streams from both hands in a circle of devastation.

"Get back!" one cried. Shrieks of terror met her ears. She forced a column of flame into the enormous skull. It cracked, then broke in two.

Blaze cut off her inner fire. Those shrieks reminded her of her own cries of terror as a child trapped in a burning house.

The ice kobolds were fleeing, rolling themselves in the snow to douse the flames that licked at their scaly hides. In full flight, their long tails lashed side to side until all were out of sight beyond the next ridge.

The fire within winked out, and the blood-red tint that had covered the world around her faded from her vision. New, brighter colors shifted into view: green pines on white snow set against a bright blue sky.

The spawning point skull flaked into cinders with a slow, satisfying hiss.

She'd won. She'd destroyed a spawning point. So the darkness could be beaten back. She had proved that much.

The Ember Mage dropped to one knee. She tried to lift her pack but couldn't. She lacked the strength. She shivered. She had spent all her heat. Suddenly even the inside of her bones felt cold. She had channeled too much heat too quickly.

She shook herself as an ashen tree collapsed in a pile of soot, entirely consumed by her last fire burst. Blaze felt just as hollow.

Must keep moving.

Her body desperately craved the softness of the snow, to simply lie down and rest.

Please. She begged her body not to give up. When night fell, the kobolds would be back and attack under cover of darkness. She needed to get as far away as possible and find shelter.

With a tremendous effort, Blaze lifted her pack. She stood and turned to continue on the path and made it several steps forward before she looked up.

Through the gap where the tree had fallen, she spied a lone figure on the rise.

It was the orc.

Chapter 5

Warrior Monk

The orc. Her quarry. Only now, she had nothing left.

She'd been so stupid. And he'd waited until after the battle—after she had spent her fire and had nothing left.

The orc was draped in a cloak; his rocklike head was bare, with twin tusks protruding up from his bottom lip. In his hand was what looked like a great club. The orc's face was marred by a tattoo that curled around his right eye.

Blaze gasped.

The Kings Summons

A Crook-Eye.

All her life she had waited for this moment, for revenge. And now she had no strength. She was at the mercy of this monster.

She stared daggers at the creature. Rage filled her. A Crook-Eye! She would fight him with her fists if she had to.

But there was no chance in that. Blaze had fought men before. Even normal human men were far stronger than a teenager like her. And this orc could toss a man as far as he wished.

The orc raised his staff and moved his arm to the side, pointing.

"This is the way. You cannot go that way," he said, cocking his head back toward what was left of the spawning point.

What? Blaze was confused. This giant orc was giving her directions?

"Hah. I won't follow you—I'm not stupid."

The orc let his arm fall. "You are tired? I will carry you." He began clomping down the rise toward her.

Blaze scrambled backward, only to trip and fall backward onto her pack, like an upturned tortoise. With his huge strides the orc was by her side before she could get free of the pack's straps.

She hadn't been so close to one of the hideous allies of the Dark Consul since that day in her village ten years ago. Now she was staring him in the face. His nose was squat and broad, his jaw wide and heavy. His head was gray, and his hulking forearms rippled with muscles, like twisted tree trunks. He reached for her with hands covered by boney spikes on the backs of his knuckles. There was an odd, misshapen lump under his cloak on one side, like he had something slung over his shoulder underneath the cloth.

Blaze lashed out with a kick.

The orc was astonishingly fast. He snatched her leg and hauled her upside down. "Why human come here?"

Blaze shivered. "To kill orcs." She couldn't tell him her true reason.

The orc turned his gaze to the still-smoking remnants of the corrupted trees surrounding the spawning point. What he had in reaction speed, he more than made up for in lack of thinking power. For a few seconds, he mulled the scene.

"You did not climb mountain—Dreck knows if being followed."

"Put me down!" Blaze thrashed to free herself.

The orc ignored her and perused the scene again. "How you get here?"

Blaze tried to swing a punch at the orc's neck, but he deftly swung her—pack and all—off to one side. "Hmmm. Fire magic scare kobolds." He looked at her, and Blaze, though upside-down, recognized how different

54

this orc was from the ones who had raided her village. His tusks were far smaller, his eyes a vibrant green. There was something almost kind in the creature's features. Blaze had to look away rather than admit it.

The orc was a magnificent creation. Powerful, like her, but somehow gentle and naive, and a slow thinker. Orcs were not stupid. But this one . . . seemed to struggle.

He dropped her on her head in the snow.

Blaze rolled to her feet and ran for it.

The orc kept pace beside her at what seemed like a brisk walk.

"Get away!" she shrieked.

The orc swung his staff, blocking her path. "Goddess send you."

"What?" Blaze couldn't believe her ears.

"Stars moving," said the orc, pointing to the sky. "Goddess is moving."

How dare an orc demon speak of the Goddess.

"Who bring you here?" he asked.

"None of your business," Blaze snapped as she desperately tried to get away.

The orc gave a snort of a laugh. "Go fast, little one. Far to go. Dreck show you."

"Little one!" Blaze scampered ahead, trying to distance herself from this strange orc. "You're not much for an orc anyway—I've seen bigger warriors."

"Dreck not warrior."

Blaze nearly tripped over her own feet. "Well—scout."

"Dreck tracker."

"A tracker—you hunt humans?" she asked.

"Tracker of great mystery. Seeker of Goddess. Dreck . . . Wandering Monk-in-training." He opened his cloak to reveal the simple brown garments of a monk. A strange, thick iron hoop hung over one shoulder and across his chest like a sling. It was covered in runes, and the iron was dark. It struck Blaze as very odd. Why would he carry something so heavy all this way? And what was it for?

But an orc-monk? "Have you lost your mind?" Blaze laughed out loud.

"Well. Dreck not monk yet. Haven't traveled to Wandering Monk Mountains. But Dreck lose self. Not mind. Dreck find peace."

Legends spoke of the time when the land of Crystalia had not known, nor feared, the Dark Consul's power. But in her lifetime, the Dark Consul's corrupting influence had reached even to the heartlands and twisted many creatures—such as the orcs—into monsters of darkness. Now none of the orc tribes followed the Goddess.

The unlikely Wandering Monk beckoned to a narrow trail that split off from the route Blaze had been following. "This way. Less travelers, less trouble," Dreck said.

Blaze was too cold to argue. Certainly, this Dreck knew where he was going. Fine. If he wasn't going to go away, she could use his knowledge of the land. She pulled her cloak tighter and fell into step beside the orc as snowflakes began to fall, covering their steps. *A Crook-Eye Orc Tracker . . . monk?*

After an hour, Dreck said, "Nice locket. Friend give you that?"

Blaze tucked the King's locket under her shirt. "Not exactly."

Blaze looked again at the much larger bulge underneath Dreck's cloak. The giant iron ring.

"My name to the Crook-Eye tribe means *big heart*," said Dreck.

"Is that your heart sticking out of your chest there?"

Dreck looked down, almost panicked, before realizing the enormous ring he wore under his robes was not, in fact, showing.

So it's a secret. That's more like it. He is hiding something.

"Does your name have a meaning?" Dreck asked.

"Of course not." She didn't know what it meant, unless *trouble* counted as a definition. "I'm Blaze." She changed the subject. "Does this path lead to Hetsa?" The village of Hetsa was on the map the king had given her. Just the place King Jasper had told her to start.

"Yes," said the orc. Now that he spoke, Blaze guessed he couldn't have been much older than her. "Hetsa, far. Enemy know fire mage come now. No use big roads. Find own road."

"All right," Blaze said, suddenly glad for the company.

"How much farther?"

The orc only opened his fanged mouth. She supposed the horrible expression was a smile.

"Don't do that . . . please."

Dreck laughed. "Goddess help you—send me."

"I don't think so. What do you know about the Goddess anyway? You're a stinking orc raider." Blaze tried to move as far away on the narrow trail as possible, but Dreck's staff-club-thing shepherded her back to the middle.

"Dreck know nothing," he said simply. "Dreck seeking path."

Blaze glowered.

"You lose staff, Ember Mage?" he asked.

"Obviously, I'm not of the Order of Ember," Blaze replied, regretting even more the company that she hadn't the strength to avoid. "Not anymore."

"You worst judge to self," said the orc.

"You don't know what I am," Blaze said.

"You sure you know?"

Blaze had no answer for that. The princess had promised her that she would become an Ember Mage. Now she'd lost that path. It had been the only one she'd known. Without it, she didn't know what she was.

"Open heart," said the monk. "Goddess will show you how to see."

It was a monk's typical mumbo jumbo. "I can't see with

58

my heart."

"Can't feel with your eyes," he said.

"Well, my heart doesn't see. It makes fire when I'm angry—I can fight ice kobolds," said Blaze.

"She make point." He gave her a gape-mouthed grin. Then he reached into a pocket inside his fur-lined gray tunic.

With the parting of his robes, Blaze caught a better glimpse of the runes inscribed into the iron ring—they had been carved into every square inch of the metal. There was something else too: what looked like a dark stone set into the metal.

A huge black diamond. There were very few black diamonds that size in all Crystalia. Wars were fought over them. Nothing was as hard as diamond—and black diamond, with its tiny aggregated crystallites, was impossible to cleave.

But Dreck closed his robes again, covering the gem and runes. He handed her what looked like a piece of bark. "Eat."

"Is it magic?" she asked.

"For some." He smiled that horrible expression again. "It's chocolate."

Blaze's eyes widened, and she bit into the frozen chocolate bar.

"Open your mouth to eat," said the monk. "Open heart to see."

"You don't understand. I lock my heart to make fire," Blaze said. "I lock in everything—anger, rage. That opens the path to the inner fire."

"And the locket," said the monk, gesturing to Blaze's shirt. "Can open that?"

Blaze drew out the locket and pried at the latch. "Stupid thing won't budge—probably broken."

"Like your heart," noted the orc.

"It's not funny. You know nothing about being an Ember Mage."

"Dreck know nothing," he repeated.

Satisfied that she had won the argument, Blaze took another bite from the chocolate. It melted in her mouth and trickled satisfyingly down her throat, seemingly filling the void left by the extinguished inner fire. "I think this stuff *is* magic."

"All is magic." He opened his arms. "You need hug?"

Blaze put up hand. "Absolutely not."

The teen orc laughed raucously loud. "You fight kobolds and afraid of hug?"

"I'm not afraid. I'm just . . ." *Angry.* She couldn't afford to let go of that. Anger lit the spark. An Ember Mage required anger—a lot of it. That didn't mix well with things like hugs and heart. But something else had her attention. A wisp of black smoke rose from behind the next peak.

"I thought this was supposed to be a rarely used trail,"

Blaze said. "I really hope you're going tell me that is a welcoming party."

"Fire not good," said the young orc. His eyes narrowed. "Stay close to Dreck."

"Are you sure you want to go this way?" Blaze said. Seeing the smoke put her on edge. They weren't alone.

"Enemy saw Blaze," said the monk. "Sure to follow. To reach Hetsa, there is no turning back."

As they hiked further into the trail that wound its way up into the towering, ice-frosted, black granite peaks of the Frostbyte Reach, Blaze found herself fighting a battle within her. Every instinct told her to reach for her magic, find the spark, store the energy, and blast this orc off the edge of a cliff.

Crook-Eye Orcs killed my parents—burned my village.

Yet, with the speed that orcs grew—even faster than humans—there was no chance this orc had been at Midway. And why did he want to become a monk?

"How long have you been a monk?" she asked.

"Five."

"Five what?"

"Five . . . happy?" The orc gave her an enormous grin.

"Five years? Five days?"

"Five days."

"I knew it. You're just pretending—what are you really doing here?"

"Dreck seek greatest mystery in Frostbyte Reach. Come.

I show you."

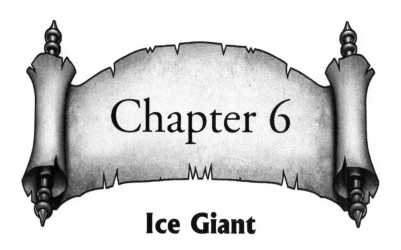

Chapter 6

Ice Giant

Blaze and Dreck spent a frigid night in a half-open cave and a solid eight hours on the trail. With each passing hour, the fire within her grew, until she knew she had enough to roast the orc.

But she didn't. Not yet. She was out of her element in the Reach. She needed him as a guide.

So long as he stays right where I can see him. She wouldn't be caught with her guard down. Not for a second. She made sure he always walked in front.

"Okay, what is this big surprise?" Blaze asked.

Dreck the monk merely nodded at the peaks and smiled.

Blaze had had a hard time finding a patch of ground to sleep on that was not covered by snow. Blaze produced her map from her rucksack and spread it in front of their meager campfire. Dreck pointed to an unfamiliar route that traced deep into the Frostbyte peaks. It was shorter by far, but likely treacherous. "This our path," he said.

Blaze winced. "Monks don't believe in the easy road?"

"What I seek is beyond all comparison," said Dreck.

Blaze smiled in recognition. *Of course.* No wonder he was going so far out of the way.

Dreck was tracking giants.

"You're going to see the jotnar—aren't you?" She said it "yote-nar" like all the dwarves she knew did. The Frostbyte Reach was famous for the ice giants that lived there.

Dreck smiled. "Long have I prepared for this journey."

The jotnar were simple beings of immense power and wisdom who spoke to outsiders only on rare occasions. Even when the orcs began their invasion of the dwarf settlements in the Reach, the jotnar did not intervene but merely retreated further into the nearly impassable mountains. Sometimes it seemed the jotnar were a world apart from mere humans.

"Dreck seek wisdom from ice giants."

The Kings Summons

"Yeah," said Blaze. He could sure use it.

Blaze stoked her inner flame just a little. Whenever she felt like igniting her spark, the orc would do something kind like take her pack or lift her over an ice flow. It was infuriating.

She had never considered how convenient it was to have a travelling companion who would soon be more than seven feet tall.

It put her on edge. Was it part of his plan? Was he trying to lure her away and ruin her chance at finding Princess Sapphire? If so, why didn't he just crush her skull in her sleep with his walking "stick" that looked more like a small tree trunk?

Out of curiosity, she gave the orc a two-handed shove toward the downhill side of the trail.

He didn't even notice.

Great. I have a boulder for a hiking companion.

The climb was unrelenting. As the altitude grew, the air lost its vigor, and Blaze was quickly out of breath. The temperature began dropping shortly after noon. She hoped her traveling cloak and the few extra layers the quartermaster was able to rummage up for her would be enough to ward off the cold. She had to focus on her mission: get in, find the princess, get out before she lost any fingers or toes to ice—or her head to orcs.

Dinner was a welcome respite. Dreck provided fresh game he'd killed in the woods, and she started the fire.

"What do *you* seek?" Dreck asked. His piercing gaze tracked her from under his pointed hood.

Blaze inched closer to their fire. The question was far harder to answer than she thought. She said nothing.

He's a monk. Monks need patience, right? He can wait.

On the third day, when the road wound alongside jagged, frosty peaks and dropped off to one side into a steep valley rimmed by evergreens, Dreck asked again. "What do you seek?"

Blaze sighed. "Nothing . . . Everything."

"It is true."

"How?"

"When your heart is closed, everything is as nothing," said Dreck.

"My heart is closed?"

Dreck nodded. "You seek to control the power of the Ember Mages, but you seek to do it alone."

"What's wrong with that? That's actually how it works, you know. You summon the spark from inside you."

"No magic is of one. It is all of Crystalia—all born of the Goddess."

Mystic mumbo jumbo.

"None of us can succeed in our journeys alone," he said.

Where have I heard that before? Blaze tucked her hands under her armpits to keep her fingers warm. "We'll see about that."

The Kings Summons

The following day, Blaze spotted more orc tracks in the snow. She said nothing about it to Dreck, who had certainly noticed the same thing. He was a tracker.

Why hadn't he said anything to her about it? Was he hoping she didn't notice—part of his tribe waiting to take her by surprise perhaps?

Blaze doubled her guard, checking every crag and looking behind as well as scouting ahead at turns when she could get ahead of Dreck's huge pace.

Her spark grew steadily closer to ignition. She wasn't going to be taken by surprise and slaughtered by the cruel creatures that had taken her parents. Thoughts of impending battle warmed her against the dropping temperatures.

"Not all magic fire from anger," Dreck said from atop a snowy ridge as he gestured to a magnificent sunset.

"Ember Magic is."

"And jotnar magic from cold hearts?" he asked.

"I guess."

Dreck gave his awful smile. "You will see." After a few hundred paces, the ridge turned and looked out over a great valley.

What Blaze saw was something she would never forget.

Far below, grand ice sculptures—great crystal pillars— rose from the steep glacial walls into sweeping ribbons and spiraling tendrils. They were grand, but at the same time delicate, like vines made of transparent stone.

The jotnar itself seemed to be made entirely of ice or living snow. It wore a short apron around its waist. The hairless skin on its bare back and chest sparkled like snowflakes in the sun.

Even from a great distance, its size was breathtaking. Its chest was huge and muscular, and its arms long enough to level a village with a few swipes.

The rays of the setting sun threaded a narrow canyon and hit the pillars, the light refracting around and between them until all were glowing with the silent fire of the setting sun.

But what came from its hands were gentle ice ribbons that twirled in arches like trestles in a garden.

Blaze gasped. She couldn't help it. In all of Crystalia, she'd never seen anything like it.

Blaze watched in silence and awe as the jotnar climbed expertly among its garden of light-scattering creations. Slowly, it drifted between ice sheets so thin Blaze could see through them like a window. Where it stepped, great platforms of ice formed like stair steps, then receded as it passed, dissolving into a blur of tiny snowflakes that drifted away in the breeze.

Despite the howling wind atop the ridge, despite the chill of her ears and nose, a serene feeling washed through Blaze—a warmth of a kind she had never known before.

"It's . . . remarkable," she whispered. But that word did not seem to do it justice.

The Kings Summons

"Jotnar magic come from whole world of Crystalia," said Dreck. Was that a tear on his cheek?

"Aren't you going to talk to it?" asked Blaze.

Dreck shook his head. He looked surprised that she would ask. "Jotnar not talk to me. What would I say?" he said. "I come here to *see* jotnar."

When they finally camped that night, Blaze slept deep, her dreams rich with twirling ribbons of ice.

She woke to a frigid dusting of powdered snow on her face.

"Ahh! That's cold." Blaze sat up expecting to see Dreck standing over her, apologizing about his big feet kicking snow at her.

Just the wind.

It was nearly sunrise, and in the dim glow of predawn, she saw something she didn't expect.

Dreck was gone.

"I knew it!" she said.

His bedding and supplies were still there. Then why had he woken so early? Orcs were famously heavy sleepers, especially when they were growing. Not as utterly oblivious as napping trolls—you could bounce a rock off a troll's face and it wouldn't notice—but close enough. Dreck was up on purpose. And he hadn't bothered to wake her.

That made Blaze feel exposed. *And now comes the ambush.*

Blaze wasted no time gathering her things. She

wrapped her cloak tightly and set off across the snow, stealing glances over her shoulders as she went.

Going backward was hopeless. The ridge ran for a mile or more, and the clear skies promised no new snow to hide her tracks. She would be spotted from a distance the moment the sun came over the horizon. Her best hope was to get ahead and get away while she could.

She tried to walk in his large footsteps but finally gave up. A Crook-Eye Tracker wouldn't be foiled by that anyway. Instead, she ran full speed ahead, charging through the snow and the bitter cold. The morning wind that crested the ridge threatened to blow her over the edge and down into the den of the jotnar. Even if it was awake, jotnar were pacifists. There was no help there.

Blessing the wind that woke her and cursing her luck at being caught by Dreck in the first place, Blaze stoked her anger. She had to be ready to summon fire in an instant.

At her first opportunity, she would break from the trail and descend the opposite slope, toward Hetsa and the populated villages of the Reach. She just needed a place that wasn't a sheer cliff. Judging by the down slope, she was approaching a saddle, perhaps even a narrow canyon.

Blaze stopped to catch her breath behind a rocky outcropping. "Come on. Just a little farther, then it's all downhill." She listened to her breath for several seconds.

A creak of metal broke the silence.

Instantly, her spark lit fire and poured into her veins.

The Kings Summons

She pressed her back against a rocky outcropping and leaned out slowly to peer across an ice field.

A hundred yards away, behind a rise and out of the jotnar's view, was a platoon of large soldiers—very large.

This was a moment for which she had prepared her entire life. "Orcs," Blaze whispered. Was this the trap Dreck had been leading her into?

How much easier was it for him to play her for the fool and make her walk the whole way herself? *No, you're jumping to conclusions*, she thought. Take a step back. She had to try to understand what was going on.

Blaze's heart beat anxiously against her ribs. There were just so many of them. Never had she felt so small and so helpless—not since Midway.

From behind a crag in the mountain, a troop of orcs hauled a great sledge. Behind them, more followed. Each sledge was loaded with cables and anchors, spears, bows, hooks, and nets of dark metal wire.

"Goddess keep us. They come to capture the jotnar," said Blaze to herself. Or corrupt it, like everything that touched the darkness. Blaze leaned out, straining to hear the commands of the orc captain.

"Get those sledges up here!" he barked. "I want everything in place when he arrives with the Iron Collar."

He? The Iron Collar. The very metal hoop that was slung under Dreck's shoulder. It was inscribed with rune magic—perhaps the work of the Dark Realm. Dreck was bringing it to them.

No wonder he had left. Now she really had to stay on her guard.

Blaze looked down into the shadowed valley where the massive giant likely lay sleeping among its creations, blissfully unaware of the danger—a giant so powerful it could trample a city in a rage or destroy an entire army.

Then there was the jotnar's magic. If legends were true, what Blaze had seen that jotnar do was just a glimpse of its power. If the jotnar became their enemy, nothing could stop them. Not even the fortifications at Dwarfholm Bastion.

Blaze gasped. "The jotnar doesn't know. I have to warn it."

But King Jasper wouldn't know of the danger either. What of him? She could go back to warn him. But he was just so far away. His forces would take weeks to get there. Blaze was on her own.

Unless . . . Princess Sapphire was in the Reach at that very moment. She could rally the dwarves. If she was alive.

As Blaze watched, another figure, this one slightly smaller, stepped slowly and carefully across the ice field that separated her from the enemy on the far side of the saddle. He joined the column of orcs ascending the slope. He stopped one of them.

Dreck.

Anger surged inside her. The traitor. Of course.

The Kings Summons

She listened as a terse conversation passed between the orcs and Dreck.

"You have that which you promised?" asked one of the orcs.

Dreck opened his robe. Even from a distance, Blaze could see the runes inscribed in the large iron ring. The black diamond was set in its center.

"Finally—you certainly waited until the last minute," said the orc. He traced his fingers over the runes. "Incredible craftsmanship. It would take years to duplicate these runes."

"The magic of the runes will be strong enough to make your dark jotnar," muttered Dreck. His eyes darted downward.

Blaze frowned, still listening. *Dark jotnar?*

The orc captain scowled. "They had better be, or Cernonos will likely have your head."

"Dreck head strong," said Dreck.

The orc captain laughed. "Crook-Eye head weak. Rimefrost Orc head twice as strong." He slammed his forehead into an ice flow and knocked a great chuck of icicle loose. "Ha! See."

Dreck said nothing to this. He simply removed his robe and lifted up his arms. Two orcs lifted the heavy Iron Collar over his head and shoulder and carried it to their sledge. They dumped it there with the rest of the metal hooks and nets.

Dreck, a traitor. And if what they were saying was true, that Iron Collar had the power to turn the jotnar into something else.

Of course Dreck was one of *them*. He was an orc to the core. Blaze shouldn't have expected anything less. She could feel her rage boiling up inside her. And with that rage came power.

I have to stop them.

But there were so many of them. If she could destroy their rune-marked weapons—it might slow their attack on the jotnar long enough for Blaze to find Princess Sapphire. Princess Sapphire would know what to do.

As the column of orc soldiers marched on, Dreck slipped away at a bend in the trail. He disappeared into the woods. Dreck the orc had chosen his path of treachery. Blaze could choose hers.

"I have the spark." Blaze said, flicking a flame from her finger. She suddenly felt so alive, so ready. "I can't let them ambush the jotnar."

She pushed back her hood. "Goddess save me."

Blaze ignited both her fists. Balls of flame enveloped them. She darted around the outcropping and dashed across the ice field toward the orcs.

She was halfway there before they spotted her. "Human!" cried one of the orcs. But it was too late, her inner heat was already surging to maximum capacity.

"Fire Wave!" A blast of superheated air jetted from her

hands, erupting in a wave of flame that spilled over the orcs hauling the sledge. Guy ropes snapped, support rails disintegrated, and snow turned to slush beneath their feet.

Shouts of panic rose up as the sledge slipped back.

But the orcs were strong. Twice the size of a man, with four times as much muscle, the full-grown warriors made Dreck look like a runt. They strained against the heavy sledge, keeping it from sliding back down the mountain with sheer muscle power.

"Stop her!" screamed the orc captain.

"Fireball!" She hurled a tight ball of flame directly at the Rimefrost Orc captain.

"Fireball! Fireball!" Blaze sent two more blasts in rapid succession. The orc captain hastily raised a shield. All three blasts deflected back toward Blaze's feet where they smashed into the snow and broke it, sizzling to nothing beneath the surface.

Blaze hesitated. The fire should have wrapped around the shield, heating it until it became too hot for the orc to hold. But the fireballs had simply bounced away.

Faint lines showed on the shield, arcane markings no living sorcerer could mimic—the work of the Dark Consul's mages.

Stupid runes, Blaze thought.

She had waited so long for a chance to face the enemy— to make them pay. To drive them back. This was the heat of battle. She couldn't stop now.

75

She lunged forward. But the ground beneath her did not hold. The snow broke and Blaze fell through.

My fireballs. They softened the snow, she thought as she tumbled down. A crevasse opened beneath her, like a great black mouth.

She scrambled for a handhold as she slid and caught on something hard and wooden. It was Dreck's staff.

"Climb!" Dreck cried as he pulled up the other side the staff.

Blaze gripped tight with both hands. She screamed, "You traitor!"

Dreck hauled her up onto solid ice. "You betrayed us!" she screamed, beating his chest with both fists.

He ignored her. "Blaze, run. Now." He pulled her behind a rocky outcropping as a hail of arrows rained down on either side. Blaze tried to catch her breath.

"Orcs have grappling hooks," said Dreck, glancing back toward the crevasse. "They cross soon. They follow."

Blaze just glowered at him. How could he?

"Here we part. You find Princess Sapphire," said the teenage orc. "I warn jotnar."

Princess Sapphire? He knew she was here? Blaze had been so careful not to mention her. She hadn't wanted Dreck to know, but he already did.

There was so much to be said—accusations, insults. And questions to ask. She had just seen Dreck deliver the key to the enemy's plans. And then he had returned to save her. It made no sense. She had to find out what was going on.

And she couldn't trust that Dreck would actually do as he said and warn the jotnar. But there was simply no time. So, she just nodded.

"Leave pack—no carry. Move quick. Follow ridge back to glacier," he said. He took the pack from off her back. She wanted to stop him, but she just didn't have the strength to resist. "Slide down. Cross river." He walked his fingers, miming the path. "Follow foot of the mountain. You find Hetsa before Rimefrost Orcs capture jotnar, turn it dark."

All depended on her success—the entire Reach. Possibly all of Crystalia.

Blaze nodded.

"Remember, cannot do alone."

This coming from a traitor orc whom she had tried to trust. She wouldn't make that mistake again.

Heart still pounding in her chest from her near-fatal fall, Blaze scurried away with nothing but her cloak on her back, sprinting back along the path. It wasn't long before darkness would fall and the brutal night chill would swallow her. A solitary thought rang in her mind. She focused on it.

Keep moving.

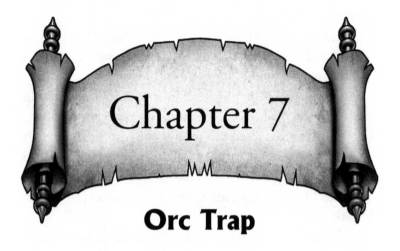

Chapter 7

Orc Trap

Howling wind blew sheets of snow across the Frostbyte Reach. The blizzard blanketed evergreens and rocks with heavy, white drifts. Gray clouds churned overhead, making angry shapes as they shot across the sky. Blaze's breath was ragged as she climbed the dunes of snow, tasting snowflakes as they blew into her mouth. Pulling her cloak around her, she shivered against the bitter cold.

"Curse you, King Jasper," Blaze muttered. It wasn't the first time she had uttered those words on this trip. And curse the orcs. It was the treachery of the Rimefrost Tribe and the Crook-Eye Orcs of the plains that gave the Dark Consul such power in the region.

And most of all, curse you, Dreck.

Soon those orcs would be unstoppable, all because of him.

Blaze trudged on. She couldn't stop now. She couldn't let them win.

The mountain path ran along the base of a steep slope that rose to her left. A gentle slope ran off to her right. Several yards ahead, an outcrop jutted out over the path, sheltering a small area from the driving snow. It was the first time Blaze had seen any actual dirt ground in what felt like days. It offered some slight protection from the growing blizzard, so she dragged herself into the space beneath the rock and blew into her hands, trying to stave off the chill.

She'd just rest for a moment. That was all she could afford. She considered lighting a fire to warm her, but it would only draw the orcs. She'd have to rely on her cloak and the rock. Besides, using fire only burned more energy. It would leave her tired, and she couldn't afford that luxury. Especially since she didn't have any food in a pack to replenish her inner fire. Making fire burned energy. Food filled her back up.

It took all her focus *not* to cast one of those wonderful warmth spells.

Without a rucksack, Blaze had no rations or blanket for the shelter. Dreck had put her in a dangerous position. How that orc made her angry! *I guess I have this,* she thought, fingering the frilly, pink locket around her neck. A lot of good that would do.

"Hetsa *must* be close," Blaze said between chattering teeth. "Didn't I just pass this bend a few hours back?" She wasn't sure if she'd followed Dreck's instructions correctly. And the blizzard was getting worse, the blowing snow cutting off her visibility to only a few feet. She had to be careful to stick to what was left of a path. It was now just a faint impression in the snow.

Blaze reluctantly stepped out from under the outcrop and forged on.

She had to warn the princess about the orcs and their plan to turn the jotnar dark, whatever that meant.

The wind howled in Blaze's ears, sending another chill down her spine. She focused on stepping through the snow banks, one frozen foot at a time.

Ahead, the path dipped down out of sight behind a ridge. Blaze focused on reaching that one goal.

Where is this dumb city, anyway? Shouldn't I have reached it by now?

When she reached the ridgetop, she gasped.

She stood at the top of a foothill overlooking a shallow valley. There, at the bottom, was a collection of burning lights—the warm, welcoming glow of lanterns and campfires. Though she couldn't see many details through the swirling snow and sleet, relief glowed within her.

"Hetsa," she said aloud.

The sight invigorated her. Picking up her pace, she half ran, half slid down the downward-sloping path. Getting a bed and a hot meal was exactly what she needed.

"Who goes there?" A voice called through the storm.

Blaze froze. She scanned the forest. The swirling blizzard and dark shadows of the evergreens blocked her view of everything but the path and the faint, glowing lights of the settlement below.

Shivering at the cold, Blaze ventured a careful response to the mysterious voice. "Hello?" she whispered.

"Who approaches our fair village?" the voice said. It was deep and guttural. "Dwarf? Freyjan?"

"Neither, actually," Blaze shouted into the storm. So this was the town guard. "I am—"

"Then orc?" the voice said.

Even above the howling storm, Blaze imagined hearing a bow drawn back. "No!" she cried. She hated how nervous she sounded. "I am a human, traveling from Crystalia Castle. I'm not from around here, but I *am* looking for Hetsa. Is that it down there?" She pointed down the pathway. The flaming lights, so welcoming to Blaze's eyes, twinkled merrily.

"Human!" the voice said. "Come, boys! Give her a welcome!"

Blaze sighed with relief as several dark figures emerged from the surrounding wood and approached her. "Oh, thank the Goddess," she said. "Here I was, thinking that I might freeze to death out here, and now you lot show up." Wrapping her cloak around her, Blaze shivered again. "I mean, look at my hands! They're nearly blue, you know. Should have brought gloves, but I didn't really think about it. I mean, it's springtime everywhere *else* in Crystalia."

"Just stay right there," the voice said. "We'll come to you." The figures emerged from the woods and circled Blaze.

The Ember Mage brushed at her cloak. The least she could do was look presentable—or intimidating—when she arrived in town. "I'm just glad Hetsa has a welcoming committee. Or are you the town guard?"

"You could say that," said the guard's voice from much closer.

Blaze tilted her head. Though she'd never actually met a dwarf from the Frostbyte Reach, she *had* met several dwarves down in warmer climates. None of them had had a voice so deep and so . . . well, guttural. *And come to think of it, these dwarves are all . . . taller than me.*

The blowing snow swirled away for a moment, and Blaze came face-to-face with six towering orcs.

Oh. Not village guards. Orcs.

Even in this raging blizzard, the orcs wore little to no clothing except for the furs draped around their shoulders and loins. Their exposed muscles bulged as they flexed and gripped their clubs, hammers, and axes. Intricate markings and tattoos covered their bodies, the white shapes reminding Blaze of storm clouds and icicles. The hulking creatures jeered at Blaze, exposing their crooked teeth. "Look. Little human can't stand the cold!" one said.

Blaze felt her lower eyelid twitch and her gut tighten. She had been running on so little sleep and was at the end of her wits. But there was more than just exhaustion.

There was anger.

Most of the orcs roared with laughter, but the orc right in front of Blaze raised his hand, cutting the others off. "Quiet!" he said. "Cernonos didn't send us to play with food. Take her to Hetsa and lock her with the other prisoners."

Blaze's arms trembled. "That was a nasty trick," she said, her voice soft and dangerous. The fire within blazed, driving the cold from her limbs. Her vision took on a crimson tint.

"Easy trick," the lead orc said, folding his arms and snorting. "Dumb human."

"Well the easy part is over." Blaze took a deep, shuddering breath. The fire within leapt up, dancing with anticipation. She would have been surprised how quickly it came, hungry and tired as she was, but she knew this fire was fueled by anger.

The lead orc snapped his fingers. "Grab her. Let's go."

83

"And you fools gave me time to charge up," she said.

The orc closest to Blaze reached down and grabbed her shoulder.

Blaze embraced the fire within.

She exploded with light.

The orc who had grabbed Blaze's shoulder fell back, clutching his charred hand and shrieking with pain. Blaze straightened her back, her body engulfed in a warm, welcoming fire that melted the snow beneath her feet. Sparks and ash joined the thousands of snowflakes swirling around the clearing. Crouching in the heat of her own flame, Blaze conjured two bright red fireballs in her hands. The orcs surrounding her took steps back, raising their muscle-bound arms and shielding their eyes from the blazing heat. The snow-covered pine trees glowed underneath the orange light.

"Just one small human!" the lead orc yelled to his men. "Do not fear her tricks!"

The injured orc roared, holding up his still-smoking hand. "She burned me!"

The lead orc snarled, revenge burning in his eyes. "Get her!"

The rest of the orcs roared and charged toward Blaze.

"Double Fireball!"

The two orcs on either side of Blaze took the fireballs, one in the face, the other in the chest. The orc who'd been hit in the face dropped his club and grabbed at his eyes. "I can't see!" The other victim clutched his chest, moaning.

The lead orc swung his ax at Blaze. She ducked under the blow and rolled through the snow away from him. Hissing steam rose into the air as the snow melted beneath Blaze's flame-engulfed body. Leaping to her feet, Blaze dodged backward to avoid getting hit by yet another orc's sword. As the orc raised its sword to strike Blaze down, she crouched in the snow, ready to spring away. The sword whooshed over Blaze's head, and she saw her opportunity. Right at the peak of the sword's arc, Blaze blasted a fireball into its tip. The weapon dislodged from the orc's grasp and spun twice through the air. The flat side smacked into another orc's face; its eyes rolled back into its head, and it fell over, limp.

"One!" Blaze shouted.

Roaring, the disarmed orc grabbed at Blaze, but she dove forward underneath its grasp and slid between its legs. The lead orc waited behind his ally. Seeing Blaze beneath him, he raised his ax above his head as if to strike her down. Thinking quickly, Blaze waved her fingers, heating up the ax handle in the orc's hands. Yelping with surprise, the lead orc let go of the ax, and it dropped from his fingers and struck his vulnerable foot. The orc let out a roar of pain and he hobbled forward, dousing his hands in the snow.

Blaze grinned. "Two!"

"Get her!" the blinded orc yelled, still rubbing at his

eyes. "What is happening?"

The orc with the scorch mark on his chest slammed his fist into his palm, revealing he wore brass knuckles. With a smirk, he leapt into the air above Blaze, his fist glinting in her own light. Blaze rolled to her right, again shooting steam into the air, as the orc hit the ground right where she'd been standing. Lighting her fists on fire, Blaze sprinted through the blizzard and struck the orc on the shoulder. His flesh sizzled, and the orc again howled.

Thud. A huge spear struck the ground next to Blaze, inches away from her. She scrambled back and saw the orc with the charred hand. Sweat beaded on his forehead, and his expression was full of concentration. He wielded his spear in an uncertain, clumsy style, proof that Blaze had scorched his dominant hand. Stepping back, he prepared to stab Blaze through.

"Thunder Strike!"

Blaze shot flame through her body into her hands. The sudden heat blast propelled her off the ground, through the air, and over the orc's thrusting spear. Flipping around in the middle of her jump, Blaze ensured her feet connected with the orc's jaw. Dazed, the orc fell like a tree, with Blaze landing on top of his face.

"Three!"

"You're done!" the orc with the brass knuckles yelled.

Blaze ducked, and the orc's fist swung over her head. With no time to turn and defend herself, Blaze sprinted off the spear orc's head and toward the edge of the clearing, where the pine trees waited amid the howling wind. Skidding through the snow banks, Blaze spun around, but the orc was right behind her.

Oh boy.

Her legs windmilling, Blaze scrambled back through the snow, desperately trying to get away from the charging orc. Her foot caught on a root, and Blaze pressed against the trunk of a pine tree.

The orc again leapt into the air, his fist cocked and ready to strike.

Grinning, Blaze curtseyed.

Wham! The orc's fist collided with the tree trunk behind Blaze. Undeterred, the orc pulled his fist back for another swing.

Whump! Snow fell in a massive pile from the pine tree, blanketing both Blaze and the orc in a world of heavy, wet whiteness. Blaze immediately melted the snow around her, her fire burning white hot. The orc himself was not so lucky; his limbs churned uselessly in a pile of soft snow. He wiggled wildly, snarling at Blaze, but she only winked and turned to run.

But heavy hands seized Blaze and lifted her aloft. "I got her!" another orc yelled, shaking her back and forth. He ran further into the middle of the clearing. "Forget Cernonos. I'm going to end her!"

Blaze tried to summon another flame to force the

orc to let her go. With some dismay, she realized the fire within had dimmed considerably. A shiver ran through her. *Blast,* Blaze thought, her mind wild. *I wasn't watching how much energy I've been using!*

The orc holding Blaze squeezed tighter. "Say your prayers, puny human," the orc said, his breath hot in Blaze's ear.

"Where is she?" a voice yelled. Blaze recognized the blinded orc's voice, coming from somewhere behind her. "I'll end her myself!"

Oh, Goddess, please let his eyesight not have come back yet.

"I'm right here!" she yelled.

Thwack!

The orc holding Blaze stiffened, then crumbled. Blaze tried to scramble free, but the heavy monster fell on top of her. With a mighty heave, Blaze pushed the unconscious orc off her legs and stood up only to be seized by the orc that had been trapped in the snow. He held her up in front of him by her collar.

"I got her!" he crowed, waving his club in the air. "Say good night."

She couldn't win a contest of strength with this behemoth. And she had only a thin thread of fire left—no more than enough for a single spark.

But not all battles were about strength. It was a matter of knowing your enemy's weak point. Hit them where they were the most sensitive.

An orc was like a mountain of muscle. It had no weak points.

But sensitive . . .

Blaze raised a finger and shot a spark into the orc's nostril.

The orc bellowed in pain, dropping her instinctively as it drew its hands toward its tender, smoking nose.

"Bye, now!" The red tint faded and the world turned back to white.

Blaze fled, leaving the orcs to nurse their wounds as she picked her way through the cover of trees toward the village below.

"Cernonos," Blaze muttered to herself. The orc captain trying to capture the jotnar had mentioned that Cernonos wanted the Iron Collar.

Who was Cernonos?—Or what?

Didn't Blaze have enough troubles already?

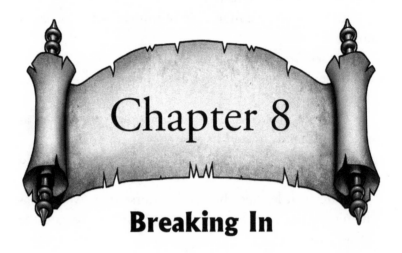

Chapter 8

Breaking In

Blaze lay on a ridge several hundred yards away from the small village of Hetsa. As she watched from afar, she felt numb. But it wasn't from the cold: the town lay in ruins.

Smoke curled over the houses. The roofs—both wooden and thatched—were charred and burned. Some of the buildings, homes, and dwellings were nothing more than ash and empty foundations.

But it was the dwarves themselves that scared Blaze.

Lines of dwarves walked through the town, heads

bowed and feet dragging. Orcs walked beside them, cracking whips and barking orders. Other dwarves, mostly youth, ran from house to house, carrying food trays or water buckets.

Blaze watched in horror as one orc took a sip of water from a dwarf boy's bucket and threw the rest in the young dwarf's face.

"By the Goddess, what happened here?" Blaze said to herself.

The orcs herded the line of dwarves into a large building carved out of the mountain. There must have been at least two dozen of them. The last dwarf, hunched over with gray hair, was a few paces behind her fellows. The orc nearest to her kicked her savagely, and she picked up her pace and scurried after the others. Laughing, the orcs slammed the door behind her. Two orcs crossed spears in front of the large building's front entrance, while the rest, looping arms and singing a war chant, paraded back out into the town. The sign outside the building read: *The Musty Beard.*

"That must be the town tavern," Blaze muttered to herself.

The young serving dwarves continued to move between houses, but now most of the dwarves carrying water and food ended up in the tavern itself. A few orcs still prowled around within the village, eyeing the young dwarves. One yelled when a youth dropped a plate of cheese in the snow.

Most of them had gone into the few buildings that were still left standing.

Blaze slid down the ridge, pursing her lips in thought. The village was lost, but what could she do? The dwarves weren't fighting. It appeared as though they had just given up. Someone had to mount a resistance.

She peeked over the ridge and caught a whiff of freshly roasted meat and frothy mead. Oh how hungry she was.

They must *be planning something.* She needed to figure out what was going on. She didn't want to do anything rash and ruin whatever plans they might have. But finding the right dwarf to give her information would be the challenge.

She could just move on. The village should solve its own problems. What did she care?

Frowning, she tossed the thought aside. She wanted to groan. There was a slim chance that Princess Sapphire was trapped in there with the rest of the villagers and that the orcs had not recognized her yet as one of the princesses of prophecy. If that was the case, then it was even more urgent that Blaze find her. *How did I get myself into this?*

Things were clearly not as bad as King Jasper had feared. They were far worse.

If the Musty Beard was where they were herding the dwarves, that was where she needed to be. Blaze studied the large structure carved out of the mountain. If there was a dwarf that she should talk to, he would be in there.

The Kings Summons

Moving carefully, Blaze continued down the foothill toward Hetsa's edge, making sure none of her footprints were visible behind her. Her cloak's velvety fringe was great for brushing her path clear.

The cloak, still coated in snowflakes, would also serve as natural camouflage against the snow-covered slope. Whenever Blaze thought an orc was staring at her, she could freeze in place. So far, no one had spotted her or raised any alarm.

Blaze stalked up to a small hut on the edge of town and pressed against the wall, her ears perked for any approaching orcs. She crept along the side of the wall, then peeked around the corner.

Now that Blaze was closer, she could see the tavern carved in the mountain in greater detail. It looked to be about the size of three dwarf-sized houses. The entire structure was one piece, with no seams or cracks across its surface. Windows gleamed within precision-cut holes, and an impressive set of double doors, complete with intricate carvings, barred the entrance. The Musty Beard was as impressive a building as any Blaze had seen. It was just what you'd expect from dwarves—building their tavern as a stronghold.

The two massive, spear-wielding orcs stood guard between her and the entrance. This is where they held the captives, possibly even important ones.

Thankfully, her hour and a half of surveillance had

given her some rest to reignite the fire within. If only she weren't so hungry. This time though, she wouldn't attack. The situation required a more subtle approach.

She snapped her fingers, producing a spark which she carefully fed into a flame as long as her forearm. Peeking around the corner again, she willed the flame toward the pair of guards.

The orcs leveled their spears at the approaching flame. Blaze bit her lip and continued to feed her inner fire into the flame. It grew larger and larger until it was as big as a large cat. Keeping it small enough was key. She had to concentrate.

"What *is* that?" one of the guards said.

"I think it's a Fire Gel," the other muttered.

Furrowing her brow, Blaze concentrated on shaping the fire into a teardrop, along with two slits near the top and a gash near the bottom. She turned up the corners of the fiery gash ever so slightly.

"Is that fire *smiling* at us?" said one of the orcs.

"That is *definitely* a Fire Gel," the second orc said.

Blaze bounced her hand up and down. The small flame turned and bounced away from the orcs, heading down the street toward a narrow building with a sign bearing a meat cleaver.

The orc's tattooed faces split wide in anger. "That Fire Gel is going to burn the meat!"

The two orcs bolted from their post, yelling and

hollering and scooping up large snow mounds as they went.

Blaze scurried to the front of the Musty Beard. Glancing behind her, she raised her arm into the air. The "Fire Gel," nothing more than a carefully crafted puppet of flame, leapt into the air and landed on the roof of the butcher shop. The thatched roof began to smolder and smoke.

"Aahhhhh!" cried one of the orcs below. "Not the meat!"

Blaze chuckled and scrambled up a pile of firewood to a window that was unlatched.

Unlatched?

Why would the Orcs leave a window to the building with captives inside unlocked?

Blaze climbed through anyway. She was about to find out.

Chapter 9

Freyr

From the window sill's vantage point, Blaze surveyed the tavern. It was massive, with seven rows of long tables lined by several dozen chairs.

Blaze didn't have long to take in the sight. The tavern was mostly empty except for a dozen or so orcs sitting near the back of the room, noisily gorging themselves on meat. She slipped off the sill and skidded across the floor, sliding beneath a table; she hoped they hadn't seen her.

The hope that she had found Princess Sapphire and

could quickly free her faded. This was going to be harder than that.

The smell of the food reminded Blaze of how long it had been since she'd eaten.

This first chamber of the tavern was not where the orcs kept their prisoners—it was their mess hall. They must have herded the dwarves into some back room. So she'd have to find that, sneak in, and free them.

Or she could get out before those orcs captured and tortured her. But the smell of roasted meat and potatoes was just *so* enticing.

Cries for help came from the orcs fighting the blaze across the street.

"Something is going on out there," one of the orcs at the table said.

Blaze crawled along beneath one of the long tables, using her elbows to prop herself up and propel herself forward.

Down at the other end of the table, an orc with bright orange feet stood, pushing away his chair. "If there is trouble with the dwarves," he said, his voice full of authority, "I'm gonna roast them."

"Ay!" the other orcs chorused.

With the thumping boots and the clanking of metal weapons, the orcs rushed out of the tavern, yelling and hollering war cries. Blaze watched their scarred, calloused feet pass before breathing a sigh of relief. The scent of fresh food and spirits filled her lungs.

There were no orc feet that she could see in any direction. She cautiously pulled herself off the floor.

The tavern was lit by candles lining the walls, casting flickering shadows across the room that kept her eyes darting from one side to the other.

She beelined for the food at the other end of the table, grabbed a ham steak, and shoved as much as she could into her mouth, chewing quickly.

"Hello," a voice said from somewhere up above her.

Blaze called upon her flame, and fire erupted from her hands. Spinning around, Blaze cocked her fists back, ready to let fly, and stopped.

A dwarf hung in a net suspended above the table by a rope tied to the rafters.

The prisoner in the net swayed slightly, spinning very slowly in circles. He twisted his body around to look Blaze in the eyes. As the net spun, he had to shift himself again to keep eye contact.

Blaze did not respond.

The dwarf tried again. "Hello there," he said. "You are well today, I hope?"

"Uh," Blaze said. "Yes?" This was not the greeting she expected. Shaking her head, she got right back into things. "Who are you? What are you doing up there?"

The dwarf sighed. "I am the Freyr of Hetsa—the mayor," he said. "But I don't recognize you as one of my flock."

The Kings Summons

Blaze shook her head. "I'm not," she said. "I'm Blaze the Ember Mage, and I'm here to rescue you. We need to arm your villagers. We need to fight!" She climbed onto the table, stepping into some of the orcs' food. "Where are they holding your guards? I'll free you and then we can rescue them."

The Freyr's expression grew frustrated. "You must *not* free me, stranger. You don't understand the situation here."

"Sure, I do!" Blaze said. She reached for the net. "You're being held captive."

The Freyr wiggled around in his net, spinning more rapidly. "That is not *all* that is happening, outsider."

"Oh really?" Blaze bent over the table and picked up a barstool. "What am I missing?"

"The orcs have my wife and children," the Freyr said. "In the backroom behind the bar."

Blaze paused. "Your family?"

The Freyr cursed, his expression growing more frustrated. "The first orc came alone, traveling with a raven on his shoulder. He was looking for a rare gem—a shining zirconia we craft deep in our mines. Looks just like a diamond but dampens magic. Said it had to be a certain cut and color. It had to be black."

That seemed like an odd request to Blaze. A black diamond. "And did you give it to him?" she asked.

The Freyr looked surprised that she'd ask. "Of course. He was willing to pay quite handsomely for it."

Adam Glendon Sidwell and Zachary James

An orc with a raven on his shoulder. That seemed odd to Blaze.

"I wish I wouldn't have! It was shortly after that the rest of the orcs arrived. They had it planned from the beginning. First, they broke into my apartment within the chambers and captured my family. They threatened their lives, telling me that if I did not bow to their wishes, my family would be the first to die.

"They commanded me to tell my village to stand down," the Freyr said, his jaw clenched. "Now they keep me here, trussed up like a bird fit to slaughter. If I disobey, then my family *will* be killed." He bowed his head as best as he could. "You must not interfere."

Blaze scowled. Blasted orcs. "There's more to it than that. There's a jotnar, and . . . the entire Reach is at stake." She didn't have time to explain everything.

"And what would you do, sacrifice your family?"

That made Blaze angry. "I don't have a family, so how would *I* know?"

But he had a point. And that frustrated Blaze. He spoke with such authority and confidence, even though he was all tied up.

He scowled. Blaze could tell she was not welcome here.

"Fine," Blaze said. "I'll free your family first."

The Freyr's eyes widened. "I will not let you risk their lives."

100

Blaze laughed. "Oh really? What are *you* going to do from up there?"

Opening his mouth, the Freyr bellowed through the Tavern. "Guards! *Guards!* Someone is trying to rescue me!"

Grabbing her head with both hands, Blaze growled at the Freyr. "Seriously?" This was why she preferred to work alone.

Blaze bolted across the table toward the front door, scattering plates and dishes. She hoped beyond hope no orc would hear the Freyr before they finished dealing with the fire outside.

Her hopes were dashed before she even reached the end of the table. The front doors to the tavern burst open, and orcs spilled into the room. "There she is!" one of the orcs yelled.

Shooting a fiery look back at the Freyr, Blaze conjured up two fireballs in her hands. "Let's go, boys!" she roared. Good thing she'd had a sandwich.

Chapter 10

Tavern Brawl

The tavern's warmth gave a welcome boost to the fire within. Blaze thrust her hands forward, shooting streams of fire at the oncoming orcs. Several fell back, throwing up their arms to protect their faces and eyes from the flame. Blaze swung her arms around, tracking the orcs who'd already run into the room to flank her. These orcs hit the ground, ducking beneath tables and chairs.

Turning, Blaze ran back toward the Freyr, blasting fireballs out of her palms behind her. The barstool she'd placed on the table still sat between her and the Freyr. The Freyr's confused look turned to shock as Blaze leapt onto the barstool and pushed off, bringing her hands forward. Her flames now extinguished, Blaze grabbed the rope suspending the Freyr's net. Clambering around, she twisted her legs around the rope and shot more fireballs at the orcs coming back inside the Tavern.

"What are you doing?" the Freyr said. "Get off me!"

"You're my shield, bud," Blaze said, blasting an orc who'd just peeked his head over the table. "This is a good vantage point."

Growling, the Freyr wriggled around in his chains. Blaze nearly lost her balance, and her next fireball went wild as she sought to regain her footing. "Stop moving around so much!" she said.

"I am *trying* to dislodge you," the Freyr said. "I will not aid you in this battle, even unwillingly!"

"Oh, don't be so hard on yourself," Blaze said. "You're doing great down there."

"You *fool*, Ember Mage!" the Freyr yelled. "Get off me at once, or I will . . ."

Thwack! An orc's club struck the Freyr in the jaw. He immediately fell limp, his loose body swaying.

"Oops," Blaze said. She glared at the orc who'd thrown the club. He had a sheepish expression on his face as he turned to look to one particular orc.

"You fool!" the particular orc yelled. "Not the one in

103

the net! The fire girl." His skin was a bright orange, though his white ice-themed tattoos remained prominent. In fact, Blaze noticed this particular orc had nearly three times as many tattoos as any of the other orcs she'd seen around Hetsa. His hair, stained red with dye and tied behind his back like some massive, dirty ponytail, was also adorned with beads and small versions of various weaponry. He wore a metal amulet around his neck shaped like a crude child's drawing of a crown.

All at once, it clicked for Blaze. *This is the orc's chief. Could this be Cernonos?*

The other orcs in the room stopped as their chief strode toward the orc who'd thrown the club. Grabbing the other, smaller orc by the neck, the chief pulled him close to his face. "You hit our prisoner, warrior," he said, red spittle flying from his mouth.

The smaller orc struggled against his chief's grasp. "I'm sorry, Chief," he said, gasping for air. "I'm sorry."

The chief dropped the smaller orc, sending him crashing into the ground. "If you're going to *throw* your weapon, warrior," he said. "Make sure you *hit* your *target.*"

With that, the chief grabbed a tomahawk off his back. Turning toward Blaze, he grinned.

"Oh, Goddess." Blaze ducked just in time as the chief's tomahawk barreled right past where she'd had her head. The weapon buried itself in the rafters behind her, quivering with a high-pitched noise.

The Kings Summons

"Get her!" the chief yelled, clapping his hands together. "She is just one puny human!"

Roaring with excitement, the orcs charged toward Blaze, leaping over tables and brandishing their weapons. Blaze shot a few fireballs, forcing several back, but the oncoming horde was too much for her to handle.

"All right then," Blaze said, slitting her eyes. Leaping from the rope, she grabbed the rafter above her and clambered up on top. Closing her eyes, she drew from the candlelight in the room, her fingers making wafting motions. The flames leapt off their candlesticks and swarmed through the air like bees, dashing in and splashing against the orcs before jumping to new targets. Confused howls filled the air as their shadows danced against the walls.

Several of the orcs were undeterred by the flame's attacks. The chief himself shrugged off the fire and leapt onto the table beneath Blaze. Leaping up, he ripped his tomahawk out of the rafter and grabbed onto Blaze's rafter. Gritting her teeth, Blaze maintained her firestorm and stomped on the orc's hand, hoping that would force him to release his grasp. The orc laughed and swung up onto the rafter to face Blaze, swinging his tomahawk with a savage grin on his face.

Blaze released the firestorm, and the entire tavern fell into darkness. Lighting her hands, Blaze shot fireball after fireball at the chief, stepping back along the top of the rafter. The orc chief batted several fireballs away, his jagged features appearing more monstrous in the brief flashes of firelight. Blaze felt her back press against a support beam, and she quailed before the orc chief's slow, steady approach. *Come on. You got this.*

Dropping her hands, Blaze crouched on top of the rafter, summoning every bit of the fire within that she had. Her entire body glowed as she held onto the power, feeding it, strengthening it.

Blaze looked across the rafter where the orc chief had stood in the darkness. "Gotcha," she said.

With that, she released the flame.

Fire exploded from within her, a blast wave of heat and flame shooting through the rafters in a circular swath. The rafters and support beams sparked, the loose bits of wood charring and smoldering beneath her attack.

But as the blast wave passed over the spot where the orc chief *should* have been, he was gone.

Blaze panicked. Something was wrong, but as she frantically reached for the fire within, it barely flickered, spent from the awesome attack she had just unleashed. *Where did he go?*

A gnarled orange hand reached out from below and grabbed Blaze's ankle. She didn't have time to react before she was ripped from her perch and thrown bodily onto the table, her body bouncing twice before sliding all the way down to the end closest to the front door. Groaning, Blaze sat up and looked toward the Freyr. The chieftain stepped around from behind the suspended dwarf. As Blaze's eyes adjusted to the darkness, the chief grinned.

He jumped off the rafter, she realized. *Dodged my blast.*

Orc hands grabbed Blaze, pinning her arms and legs with her back against the table. Laughter filled the tavern as the orcs surrounded her, their darkened expressions mocking and jeering. Blaze struggled to free herself, to roast the orcs, to do something, *anything*, but she was too weak, and her flame was still dim.

The orc chieftain stood over her, tossing his tomahawk in his hands. "Puny human," he said. "You thought yourself a Hero? Look at you now, lying there, weak as a kitten." He laughed, and the other orcs joined in. "It is over, Ember Mage."

Blaze cast her eyes everywhere, looking for a way out. *Please, Goddess! I don't want to die!*

"You challenge Rimefrost Orcs," the chief said, gripping his tomahawk in one hand. His crown-shaped amulet dangled against his bare chest. "You choose death."

She was pinned. There was nothing she could do to direct what little flame she had remaining to take out one of the orcs, let alone all of them.

The chief raised his tomahawk over his head to bring it down upon Blaze. "Cernonos will be pleased."

In her last moments, Blaze thought of King Jasper. *I'm sorry I didn't find Princess Sapphire, Your Majesty.* She

107

closed her eyes. *I failed.*

A great crash sounded.

Bits of broken glass from the nearest window peppered the orcs. As her captors reflexively raised their arms to shield their eyes from the hail of shards, Blaze was momentarily free.

She rolled off the table and scrambled toward the window that had crashed. As a gust of winter wind whipped through the broken window, a huge hand reached down for her.

I recognize those hands.

"This one is mine," said the orc that had shattered the window.

"It's a Crook-Eye!" bellowed the orc chief. "Stop him!"

"Get the Goddess-loving traitor!"

Blaze barely had time to scream before Dreck had tucked her under his arm and leapt out of the window.

Blaze was airborne as Dreck tossed her ahead. Then the orc teen raised a massive, oversized barrel, his muscles and veins bulging as he hurled it at a pair of pursuers. A great cloud of white powder filled the alley.

Blaze almost laughed. *Too easy.* She drew a spark and let it fly.

Dreck was just passing her as the sparks lit the powder. The clouds of dry-milled flour went up in a burst of flame like gnomish musket powder.

The detonation blasted Blaze back off her feet.

The Kings Summons

All went silent. Her eyes filled with a great white spot. Suddenly, she felt Dreck's shoulders under her hands. She gripped the knobby bones protruding where his neck met his shoulders and rested her weight onto his back.

Why was he back now? What did he want? Suspicion gnawed at her mind.

Dreck was not the biggest orc, but there was no question the Wandering Monk was the fastest orc she had ever seen.

Dreck blitzed through the darkness as barely visible tree branches whipped past. He slowed only to pick something up off the ground.

Was that her rucksack? He'd saved it.

But what was he doing here now? He was supposed to have been warning the jotnar. Or was that just another thing he'd said that she shouldn't have trusted?

And she had fallen for it. In the heat—or the cold—of the moment, she had trusted him. She had left the warning of the jotnar to him—the very person who had delivered the Iron Collar to the Rimefrost warriors preparing to ambush the unsuspecting jotnar.

Blaze had little time to worry about that. With the fire of battle quenched, she fell into the aching cold of ember exhaustion.

Even atop the back of the charging orc, whose hot breath came in heaving gasps, cold seeped through her clothing. She shivered so powerfully she could barely hold on.

"Dreck," she said, realizing that her voice sounded even weaker. "I'm freezing."

"Not much farther," he said.

"I can't hold on."

"Open locket—find strength."

"How do you—" King Jasper had told her it would open only when she was twice her normal strength. That certainly wasn't now.

"No time," Dreck said.

Squeezing Dreck's waist with her legs, Blaze reached for the locket under her shirt. He had saved her—again. Was it possible that she really could trust him? She wanted to hate him for everything he'd done. But right now, she just couldn't muster the strength.

The locket opened a crack, and a tiny sliver of light shone through. A thrill of warmth and energy rushed into her body. She recalled holding her Ember Staff, conjuring flames in a circle around her in an underground lava cavern near the molten core of the volcano. The memory enveloped her.

She stared into the locket, willing it open further. *Twice my strength.* But seconds later it snapped shut again. The warmth faded.

Dreck plunged through snow drift after snow drift at incredible speeds. He leapt from tall boulders and across the icy waters of a narrow ravine. As the miles of snowy forest passed, and the night raced on, Blaze grew steadily colder. The strength of the locket passed as quickly as it had come. The ache of chill and uncontrollable shivers returned.

"Please," Blaze said, her voice cracking as though at the verge of tears. "I can't . . ."

"Not long now."

It was almost dawn—the coldest part of the day—when suddenly Blaze felt a pocket of warm air. As light kissed the horizon, Blaze spied vapors drifting through a small rocky clearing.

Not a spawning point. Not now. She didn't have the strength. "Is this a spawning point?" she whispered.

Dreck shook his head. "No."

The air was damp and warm. Water trickled between the rocks. A strange quiet hung in the air.

"Secret place," Dreck said. "Sacred Spring of the Goddess—heal you."

A blazing sunburst lit the heavens, stretching from one horizon to the next, streaks of yellow light knifing their way across the sky.

Dreck crouched and Blaze fell to the ground. The damp rock was not cold to her touch like she'd expected.

Dreck fell to his knees, his hiking staff clattering as it rolled a pace away. He pushed the pack toward Blaze as she shivered.

The morning light cracked between the trees and lit

a crystal, steaming pool. Blaze shuddered with a sudden thrill.

Of all the glorious flame and fire . . .

"Hot springs!" she said.

Chapter 11

Snow Goblins

Cascading pools of turquoise water tinged with orange and green around its edges flowed through a breathtaking oasis of life. Ferns curled over smooth granite stones, and moss softened the ground.

Blaze reached out and dipped her hand into the nearest pool. It was just shy of scalding—but so hot, the mere touch of the water ran into her like liquid energy.

Blaze opened her rucksack and dug through her personal gear at the bottom. She pulled out her standard-issue, red Ember Mage bathing suit and stepped behind a broad fern to change.

Blaze returned to see Dreck seated cross-legged, leaning his back against a pine tree, staring into the pools of water.

She'd never noticed before how different his dark green tattoos were from the Rimefrost Orcs' white, ice-themed tattoos. Most of Dreck's were shaped like trees, leaves, or other plant life. Blaze could trace a distinctive vine trailing around the orc's eyes and around his neck. For whatever reason, the design made Dreck look softer. Far softer than any of the other orcs she'd encountered.

Was he really so different from them? He seemed to want to be.

Not wanting to damage Princess Ruby's locket, Blaze removed it and tucked it into the outer pocket of her pack. Then she tiptoed into the pool and sank into the luxurious, bubbling spring water.

"A. Maze. Zing." She sighed.

"Sacred pool give life," Dreck said.

"You aren't . . . getting in?"

"Dreck waiting."

"For . . ."

He closed his eyes and his breathing became deep and slow.

He's asleep.

Blaze had the sudden impulse to grab her things and run. Sure, he had saved her *again*. But why? It seemed

114

that their goals here in the Frostbyte Reach were entirely opposite. Dreck had delivered to the enemy this strange Iron Collar that they said they needed to enslave the jotnar. Did he want a dark jotnar unleashed on all of Crystalia? What would he do if he found Princess Sapphire? Blaze would need to protect her from Dreck at all costs.

Besides, how was she going to hide from an orc tracker with a nose like a bloodhound and legs just as fast?

She *needed* to confront him about the Iron Collar. She would when he woke up.

For the moment, she needed to let the hot water soak into her bones. It was almost as if she could feel the energy radiate from deep within the core of Crystalia.

After more than an hour, she hoisted herself up to the edge of the pool and dangled her legs in the water. She pulled out some supplies from her pack: a few dried figs and what tasted like moose jerky.

From across the pool, a small, green face with an enormous nose and set of tiny eyes peered out from behind a tree.

"A goblin!" said Blaze.

The green, helmeted creature darted behind the rock nearest Blaze and stuck its face out, its eyes focused on the food in her hand. "You want some?" Blaze held out a small piece of fig.

The goblin made a soft grunt of interest and climbed onto a branch, then leapt across the pool to a branch near

Blaze. It dangled from one arm and reached for the snack.

"You're so cute."

Blaze offered the fig to the goblin, only to catch a flash of red cape as another goblin pulled her food pouch off her lap and hauled it away into the trees, shrieking with laughter.

Blaze jumped to her feet. "Give that back! That's my food."

Two more goblins dropped from the trees. One landed on the ground, scooped up a stone, and flung it at her. It sailed dangerously close to her head.

"Knock it off!" she cried.

She spun to see another goblin hauling away a pair of her underclothes.

"Hey! Those are mine."

She managed to snatch her clothes, only to have another stone hit her in the rear. She spun around to catch the culprit, just as the first goblin leapt down, reached into the outer pocket and pulled out Ruby's locket.

No!

With a snicker of delight, the goblin bounded back up a tree. It waved the shining locket and then jumped to a higher branch.

"Give that back—Dreck, help!"

She turned.

He was gone.

Was this one of his tricks? To lure her here and abandon

her to these creatures?

Blaze conjured a fireball from pure rage and cast it at the nearest goblin with both hands. The creature dodged it easily and fled deeper into the snowy woods with the rest of its troop.

Blaze looked at the mess around her. Her clothing was strewn through the mud. Her food all but gone. Her socks dangled from a branch she couldn't reach.

And Dreck was gone.

Blaze collapsed onto the ground. Her perfect moment was ruined. Everything was ruined. Dreck had gone again—maybe for the better. Maybe he'd led her into this trap.

Was the locket really that important?

Was he working for the Dark Consul—a spy?

And he knew about Princess Sapphire.

Blaze started to pick up her things but couldn't find the heart to finish. She broke into tears.

Why was all this happening? She had to pull herself together. She was *Blaze*.

She wiped her tears away and looked up to see the orc monk standing several yards away.

"You!" she cried. She charged him, beating uselessly at his rock-like abs. She swung several punches at his ribs. It hurt her knuckles far worse than it probably hurt Dreck.

"Where were you! Where is my locket?"

"Big go behind tree."

"Big go?—You gave them the Iron Collar!" she shouted. "You're working for *them!*"

Dreck's brow wrinkled down over his eyes. He looked angry. "What you know about Iron Collar?"

"That they're going to use it to enslave the jotnar—and it's your fault," she said. She was going to let it all out now.

Dreck blew a blast of hot air out of his nostrils. He threw off his monk robe. "No. You puny mage. You no understand plans for Frostbyte Reach." He cracked his knuckles.

What, was he going to fight her? Blaze didn't care. He had this coming. "And then the goblins you lured here just stole my locket!"

Dreck's expression shifted. "Goblin steal your locket?"

"Yes, you big buffoon."

His big hand reached across and pointed at the mud on her chest. "You take mud bath like orcs?"

"Get away from me!" Blaze retreated back toward the pool. "Just get away!"

Dreck turned and stalked away. For a moment, it was silent.

Choked by emotion, Blaze dove back into the pool, hiding the tears that flowed freely in the warm water of the sacred spring. In minutes, her body was clean, but she didn't feel clean. Something clung to her insides, a feeling she couldn't wash away so easily.

The Kings Summons

"Come on, Blaze. Princess Sapphire is counting on you." The Ember Mage changed back into winter clothes, lit a small fire to ward off the cold—and so she could watch for goblins—and lay down.

She woke hours later with the sun high overhead. There was still no sign of Dreck. Probably better that way.

Her stomach rumbled, but she had nothing to help with that. She needed to find another settlement, somewhere the orcs hadn't already taken over—somewhere bigger than Hetsa.

She spread her map on the ground—luckily the goblins hadn't taken any interest in it—and drew a line from Hetsa to the nearest city.

"Foruk's Falls." It was a day and half's journey. "I can do this."

She would have to go fast to keep the orc monk from following her steps.

Blaze took her bearings from the sun, shouldered her pack, leaving behind the extra socks she couldn't reach, and tromped into the snowy woods.

"If I see a goblin . . .

"Eating my food . . .

"Wearing my underwear . . ."

But she was too tired to draw a spark. All she could do was fume.

A large raven landed on a branch not far away, watching her with dubious eyes.

"And what do you want?" she said.

"Cah!"

"Same to you!" Blaze said. A raven . . . something about a raven was important. There was something she should have remembered. But what?

The bird took to wing, heading in the direction from which she had come.

"And good luck with the goblins. They'll rob every feather off your body!" she shouted after it.

She just *had* to make it to Foruk's Falls.

Chapter 12

Snow Bear

The city of Foruk's Falls lay nestled at the base of an enormous granite mountain far below her. It was at least a day's journey.

Blaze had traveled as far as she could for the day. Now she sat, huddled as close to the firepit as she could, shivering even as warmth filled her body. Lighting a fire always gave her more heat than if she summoned all that flame herself. That way she could absorb heat instead of use it up. Better to burn wood than burn up her inner flame.

The dense pine trees kept the howl of the mountain air down to a stiff breeze. The clouds had broken up above, and the moon was visible through the treetops, though wind gusts still guided snow flurries through the sky.

She had to stay on her guard. She imagined orcs creeping through the woods just out of sight, having followed her out of Hetsa. Throwing her hood over her head, she peered out into the darkness.

"I am back," Dreck said behind her.

With a scream, Blaze summoned fireballs to her hands. The fire in the pit exploded upward, a pillar shooting into the sky. Gasping for breath, the Ember Mage whirled around and glared at the orc. "Don't do that!"

"Do what?" Dreck asked.

"Sneak up behind me like that! I didn't even hear you!"

Dreck shrugged. "Son of Crook-Eye Tracker. Make no sound." He stepped around Blaze and set down a large stack of branches by the fire. He added a few branches and sat across the crackling flames from Blaze.

He was quiet. For some reason, that infuriated Blaze. *What does he want—an apology?*

A hug?

He was *not* getting a hug. After minutes of painful silence, Blaze spoke. She wanted to find out more about the Iron Collar, but what good would it do? He wasn't going to tell her. And if she pressed the issue, Dreck might even go so far as to kill her. She didn't know what the orc would do.

"How did you find me?" she asked. She stared at the orc.

Dreck stoked the fire with a stick, frowning in apparent thought.

It was as if *he* didn't trust *her*.

It only made her want him to speak more.

He held out his oak-branch arm and gave a low whistle.

A large, black shape swooped down toward Dreck, claws outstretched. Blaze flinched and lit her palms on fire, ready to blast the creature. Dreck looked up and smiled. The black shape landed on the orc's shoulder in a flurry of feathers. Cawing softly, it nuzzled its head against Dreck's ear.

"The raven," Blaze said, extinguishing her flames. "It's yours?"

The orc looked over at the bird. "Raven is friend of Crook-Eye Orcs—raven see far."

"I saw it earlier in the day," Blaze said. She didn't mention she had yelled at it, and thankfully, neither did the bird.

He indicated a band on the bird's leg. "This bird called Rav."

"Rav the Raven. Whose brilliant idea was that?"

"My father."

Blaze clamped her mouth shut. Then she remembered.

The Freyr of Hetsa had said an orc with a raven had scouted out the village just before the rest of the orcs invaded. He'd come looking for a gem—a black zirconia. It had to be Dreck.

"What were you doing in Hetsa before the attack?" she asked. She pointed a flaming finger at him. "I know you were there. Dreck, did you lead the orcs into Hetsa?"

Dreck didn't even look up at her. "Rav bring news." Dreck unrolled a small piece of paper with markings Blaze could not recognize. The scrap was small enough to be wrapped on the crow's leg.

"Dreck, listen to me. Why did you want that zirconia from Hetsa? What was it?"

Dreck smashed his foot into the ground. It felt like the ground shook. "No!" he said. His nostrils flared, and his hot breath turned into vapor in the cold.

Blaze took a step back. She didn't know he could get so furious. For a moment, she wondered if he would attack.

"No, Ember Mage!" growled Dreck. He balled up his fists. "No secrets for Blaze."

She'd pressed him too hard. But why? What was he hiding? So it *had* been him at Hetsa. And there was something important about that gem. She needed to find out. But not now. Fine. If he wouldn't trust her, she couldn't trust him.

Dreck slowly unclenched his fists. His shoulders slumped. He looked away. He looked ashamed.

The Kings Summons

"Read message," he said, looking down at the scrap of paper. He was trying to change the subject.

Fine. She'd play along. For now. "What does it say?" she asked.

"Foruk's Falls captured," he said.

Blaze's heart sank. "Oh no."

"Crook-Eye Orcs now come to Frostbyte. Come to help Princess."

"What?" That made no sense. So he *did* know Princess Sapphire was here. But why would Crook-Eye Orcs—the very tribe Princess Sapphire had defeated so long ago in Midway—come to help her? They were mortal enemies.

"Princess ask chief for help. Chief bring warriors to the Reach," he said.

"So that's where she was all this time—asking for help from a troop of raiders?" Blaze let off a quick burst of heat from her fists. Now she really couldn't hold back her temper. None of this sounded right. It just didn't sound like Princess Sapphire. "I can't believe a word of this."

"Truth," said Dreck.

"Do you even—do you know why I don't believe any of this?" Blaze boiled. The heat was rising in her again. She stood up, barely taller than Dreck seated. "Because *I* was there."

She wanted to scream but didn't dare draw attention. If Foruk's Falls was near, so was the enemy. "I was there, Dreck. *I* was in Midway."

The young orc's expression didn't change.

"And I was the only survivor."

Dreck tucked his lip under his teeth and looked at the ground.

"The only reason I survived was because Princess Sapphire fought off a whole pack of Crook-Eye Orcs to save me. So, don't try to tell me that Princess Sapphire is friends with a bunch of—" Blaze was so angry, she couldn't even speak, so angry she didn't dare light the spark for fear of burning herself up.

By the end of her tale, tears had formed into ice crystals on the corners of Dreck's eyes.

Blaze felt empty.

And why was *he* crying? It was her story, her pain, not his.

The great orc shook with low sobs.

Oh great. Why was he doing this? Why did he think he got to be the victim?

Blaze turned up her hands. He just made her so . . . angry. She hadn't felt so angry in years. "Dreck, what do you want—what am I—" She found words coming out of her mouth without her permission. "What, you want a hug?" she roared.

He nodded. He looked so pitiful, his lower lip trembling.

"Hhhh." Blaze let out a breath. He'd stopped her in her tracks. She groaned in frustration. She took three quick steps toward him, then turned back. Maybe she should light him on fire instead.

"This is not a good idea."

"I share story," Dreck said.

"No. We need rest. I'm tired. Tomorrow we have to find Princess Sapphire," said Blaze.

"Meet Princess Sapphire at Black Blood Peak," said Dreck.

"What?" Blaze spun back.

Dreck lifted the paper with illegible markings. "Find Princess at overlook near Cernonos war camp."

Yeah right. That didn't sound like a trap.

But what if Princess Sapphire really was that close? Even if he was lying, even if this was all a trap, if there was even a chance of finding Princess Sapphire, Blaze would go.

Silence settled between Dreck and Blaze as the winter winds swept between them. Rav nestled deeper into the orc's shoulder, tucking its beak into its wing.

Several things needled Blaze, things that didn't match up. First of all, the convenience of a young monk running into his tribesmen at one particular point deep in the massive Frostbyte Reach. The black zirconia. The Iron Collar. And even more unlikely was Dreck's claim that Princess Sapphire was in league with orcs—especially Crook-Eye ones.

Dreck had walked past the spawning point when she'd

first arrived in the Reach, yet it hadn't triggered.

And why had he arrived at Hetsa so soon after her? And before her. Had he led the orc invaders there?

She had to find answers. Both her life and the princess' were at stake—which meant all of Crystalia.

"You were supposed to be warning the jotnar," Blaze said. "That was your job. I needed you to do that."

"You need sleep," Dreck said. "Wake early tomorrow."

"Don't avoid the question."

"Caw!" said the raven.

"You stay out of this, Rav. I'm still not sure whose side you're on, Dreck. I don't know what to think."

The campfire fizzled out. Blaze's burst of emotion had drained all of its flame.

"Blast it—I didn't mean to do that," she muttered.

"Blaze only open ears. Can't hear. Can't see." Dreck gestured with his oversized fingers, touching the pointed stubs of his own ears and his heavy-lidded brows.

"What don't I see?" Blaze said. "Tell me."

Dreck reached into his robes. Blaze flinched. The orc drew out two thin objects and lay them on the ground, and for a brief, fleeting moment, Blaze thought they were snakes.

"Oh—it's just my socks." She gave a sigh. "Thanks." It was like dealing with a toddler. She wanted to have a serious discussion about his loyalties, and he was—"What are you doing?"

The Kings Summons

Dreck stamped on the ashes, spreading the dimly flaring coals. He kicked a shallow layer of dirt over the coals. "Sleep here—stay warm."

Blaze reached down and touched the earth. It wasn't hot, but she could feel warmth trickling up. "Good idea." She rolled out her bedroll on the coals and lay down, but sleep wouldn't come with her conscience pricking at her.

"Dreck," she said. "Where are you sleeping?"

He gestured haplessly around the camp, then lay down on the bare dirt with only his monk's robe underneath and pulled a large fur blanket over him—it only reached halfway down his legs, leaving his toes bare.

"What about your toes?" she asked.

Dreck sat up and looked at them. "What wrong with toes?"

"Can't you sleep with your boots on?"

"Feet grow at night. Big pain."

Blaze retrieved her socks, then tossed them at Dreck. "Here, put these on."

He pulled one and then the other onto his feet. They only stretched halfway up his foot. The socks strained to the point of ripping—they would never be the same after this.

"Oh!" he said, wiggling his toes. He pointed at his feet. "That nice."

Nice.

The strange word hit Blaze like a punch to the stomach.

129

I hope I know what I'm doing.
Like magic, sleep took her.

She woke to the smell of roasting fish. "Elegant elbows of the Goddess! That smells great."

Blaze sat up, pushing off not only her blanket but also an extra fur blanket, the same one Dreck had used the night before.

No wonder I slept so well.

"Eat on trail." Dreck handed her a stick with a fish stuck on the end.

Blaze bit into the crispy trout and pulled the soft meat away from the tiny bones. It was plain food, but warm. She needed that.

Dreck bit the head off a large catfish and then downed the rest of it in two bites.

A goliath catfish like that would have fed an entire gnome family for dinner.

Dreck must have fished downstream from the hot springs, she realized . . . *After finding my socks.*

No wonder he was slow catching up.

Blaze stuck her fish-on-a-stick in the snow while she folded her bedroll and loaded her pack.

Dreck tucked her toe-warmer socks in the top.

"You keep those," Blaze said. The idea of sweaty orc-feet socks in her pack was all too disturbing.

The Kings Summons

Dreck nodded and tucked them into a hip pack that he tied around his waist before donning his monk's cloak, retrieving his staff, and stomping out his cooking fire.

Blaze lifted her pack and finished her breakfast on the trail, jogging to keep pace with Dreck.

Today she was going to find Princess Sapphire. She was almost going to complete her quest and return the princess to King Jasper safe and sound.

If the orc's crow-born intelligence was correct. And if this wasn't a trap.

Orc intelligence. She was relying on orc intelligence.

Still, she kept up hope that as ridiculous as the idea seemed, perhaps Princess Sapphire really was travelling with Crook-Eye Orc raiders from the foothills of the Frostbyte Reach.

"What about the jotnar?" Blaze asked. It was worth trying to pry information from him again.

"Jotnar ignore Dreck—like insect," said Dreck.

So, he had tried to warn the jotnar after all?

"What? You're huge. That thing just—"

"Jotnar not bothered by small problems. So, Dreck track Blaze to Hetsa."

"Track me—in the middle of the night. How?"

He pointed to his face. "Orc nose."

"You smelled me?"

"Perfume on locket. Soot on hands. Leather on boots. Moose jerky in pack. Figs. Stinky socks. Not brush teeth in many days. Mouth stink like orc."

"Got it. You can smell. But the jotnar—it's still in danger. How close are the orcs to it?"

The memory of Dreck handing over the Iron Collar stabbed at her.

"We must hurry," he said.

"Is there any way to get a message to the princess about the jotnar?"

"You bring pencil?"

"Uh . . . no."

Dreck shrugged.

"I get it, the raven can't talk. But there has to be a way—"

"Not now. Must be careful. Cernonos watching," he said.

"Everyone keeps talking about Cernonos. But who is he?" asked Blaze.

"Big demon. Come from dark magic. Servant of Dark Consul," said Dreck. "He rally Rimefrost Orcs. He the one try to enslave jotnar."

"Then how do we—"

Dreck raised his arm and stopped mid-stride, like a stork on one leg.

Blaze froze. She knew better than to ask. His posture and raised arm told her now was not the time.

Dreck moved his body almost imperceptibly until the toe of his boot touched the ground. Seconds later, his heel came to rest silently in the snow.

Then the sounds of tramping feet, huffing, and low grunts moved through the trees.

My bright blue cloak—they'll see me.

But Dreck did not so much as move his head or whisper a word of warning.

Blaze was desperate to hide. Was this part of the trap? Had he forgotten she was wearing a blue cloak? She felt like a sitting duck.

True, he wasn't the brightest.

Heart pounding within her, Blaze listened as the sounds of orc warriors drew closer.

Dreck drew in a long slow breath and held it.

He did that on purpose—hold my breath. Got it.

Blaze took in a breath and held it as the line of orc soldiers marched across the trail, heading uphill.

Toward Black Blood Peak.

Each beat of her heart thundered in her chest, the desire to gasp for air was like a hammer beating on her lungs.

But the orcs kept coming, dozens upon dozens.

From Foruk's Falls, Blaze realized. Dreck had said the city was captured, so why were so many of this demon Cernonos's forces retreating?

At last, the final orc soldiers passed. Two scouts brought up the rear, their eyes scanning as they sighted down their half-drawn bows.

They'll see me.

The orcs turned slowly. One tilted its head as it looked right at her.

A chill ran down into Blaze's heart.

The orc sniffed, then moved past and into the cover of trees uphill.

Desperate for air, Blaze let out her breath and took in a gasp of chill Frostbyte air.

How is that possible? Why didn't they see me?

After several minutes Dreck turned to look at Blaze. He smiled.

"My blue cloak?" Blaze said. "How did they not see me?"

"Orc not see blue—black as coal."

"Orc eyes not so good," Blaze said, using Dreck's broken language. "See with nose."

He nodded.

Apparently, they didn't have birds to scout for them either. "So the Rimefrost Orcs don't have ravens?"

He nodded again.

"Rimefrost Orcs ride snow bears."

"Snow bears? They see better?"

He laughed. "Bear smash better. Kill better."

"Oh great." She shuddered at the thought of a bear large enough for a hulking orc to ride.

They resumed their cross-country trek toward the valley overlook on the backside of Black Blood Peak. "The orcs were coming from Foruk's Falls," she whispered. "Why were they going back to the war camp?"

"Dreck think big thing happen."

"Wonderful."

"Not wonderful. Big thing bad."

Blaze rolled her eyes. "That's not what I meant." Her sarcasm was entirely lost on Dreck.

Dreck lifted Rav from under his cloak and let the raven take to wing.

"Where is Rav going?"

"Find father. Find Princess."

The pair resumed their trek, jogging now. Past noon, as hunger returned to taunt her, Dreck suddenly said, "You want bread?"

"What bread?"

"Here," said Dreck, handing her several flat loaves of hard bread from his pack.

Without time for a fire to boil the barely edible, rock-like loaf, Blaze took a handful of snow in her hands. "Put the bread on top," she said.

Dreck place the bread onto the snow in her hands.

Come on, fire. I need you.

A different sort of spark tried to rise up in her but failed to ignite. "Come on!" Anger rising to meet her hunger, the world flashed red, and then her hands coursed with heat.

The snow flash-melted and boiled the bread.

"Wow. Ember Mage cook in hands. Never see," said Dreck.

"Yeah, I just made this up."

The hard loaf softened and rose, plumping into a loaf that glistened as the last drops of water sizzled away. Blaze took a piece and handed the rest to Dreck. "One loaf a day—standard rations."

"Pitiful ration," said Dreck.

"Sorry."

Dreck wolfed the bread down in a single gulp.

"Ten pounds meat standard orc rations."

"Good grief," she sighed.

Dreck shrugged.

Her stomach no longer growling for food, Blaze and Dreck returned to their tortured pace. The trail steepened as the sun dipped toward the western horizon.

Dreck took her pack and slung it over one shoulder. Blaze was too tired to protest.

That's everything I own. He better not lose it.

With the temperature dropping, Blaze thought wistfully of the hot springs.

I could almost tolerate those horrible goblins.

Almost.

Ever wary, Blaze could not ignore the fact that every place to which Dreck had led her turned out to be a disaster, if not a baited trap. First there was the spawning point, then the orc jotnar-capturing party, Hetsa, the

goblin thief's guild at the hot spring, and now . . .
Black Blood Peak.

It all came down to this. She had to get Princess Sapphire back to safety. Whether or not the war in the Reach succeeded, the prophecy could not fail. The Goddess's last words as she bound her essence to the Dark Consul to force him out of Crystalia had been the prophecy of the five. They were the only ones who could end the conflict.

For years it had seemed the Dark Consul was gone. But by the time his spreading network of spawning points was discovered, it was too late.

Everyone knew the Dark Consul himself could not enter the realm of Crystalia—not while he was still bound by the Goddess's essence—but his invasion continued through the hands of power-hungry magicians. The loremasters often spoke of the infamous Ikalos, whose meddling had merged the Nether Realms and Crystalia in the region surrounding the Midnight Tower.

Once enough of the entire realm had been taken by the darkness, there would be no barrier of Goddess-born light to hold him back. He would return, and all of Crystalia would fall to corruption, evil, and destruction.

His return was imminent—so said the loremasters. And when he did, all faced their doom, unless the five defeated him—all five, Princess Sapphire included.

Yet what of the dwarves who would fall to the ice

giants Cernonos was trying to corrupt? Should Princess Sapphire abandon them to save herself?

Logic said yes.

But what would the Goddess want?

Ask the monk.

Right.

"So," Blaze said. "In your five days of training—or however long you studied, since time doesn't seem to be your strong suit—did you discuss whether the Goddess would rather let a bunch of innocent people die to save one, or save as many as possible and then doom everybody?"

Dreck's already heavy eyebrows furrowed even deeper, like ledges overhanging two caves where his beady eyes stared ahead blankly.

That's a no.

"Dreck learn Goddess's will is not destination. Must follow path."

"Great," she said lamely. "I'll keep that in mind next time I have to make a decision that might just doom all Crystalia."

"Wandering Monk not walk path to be alone. Walk path to find others."

Blaze felt like someone had just dumped a bucket of cold water on the furnace of her thought forge.

"Like weaving cloth. Find Goddess in the pattern, not thread," said Dreck.

"Come again?"

The Kings Summons

"Weave thread together, we survive. Save thread, lose blanket."

"Ok, that's gonna take some time to sink in," Blaze muttered. For a long time, Blaze tried to put the orc's infectiously ignorant thoughts out of her mind. But each time she turned them over in her head, she found only sands of confusion slipping through her fingers.

"Once upon a time," Dreck suddenly began.

"Oh good, a bedtime story," Blaze toned sarcastically.

"Not bedtime. Just story."

"Got it."

"Orc raiders burn village."

"Heard this one before—I was there, remember?"

"Dreck father there," said the orc.

That was a surprise. And not a welcome one. A pit formed in Blaze's stomach.

"Dreck father fight Princess Sapphire. Dreck father fall."

Blaze's heart seized up. Dreck's father was one of the four orc warriors who had attacked Princess Sapphire!

"Princess fight but not kill. Princess stop soldiers. Let orcs go."

The words felt like a stab to her heart. "What?"

"Princess show Crook-Eye tribe way of Goddess. Not cut thread—weave together."

Blaze was speechless. This whole time she had wanted revenge on the orcs for raiding her village, thinking

Princess Sapphire to be her savior—the one who defeated them. But Princess Sapphire had let the murdering orcs go—LET THEM GO! She must have stopped the king's cavaliers from running them into the ground.

Why?

Blaze's head spun. Her palms sweat. Heat trickled up her spine. The world went a light shade of red. The inner spark had lit without her permission. Now it filled her.

She didn't want it.

The inner fire grew. To dangerous levels beyond her control.

"Blaze look hot," said Dreck. He looked scared.

"That's what all the boys say," she said, a twinge of pain stabbing her heart. Her joke fell flat. But it had worked. The fire connection short-circuited. Blaze let the rage pass. She stumbled forward, burying her hot hands in the icy snow.

Tears melted down her cheeks.

She was crying at his story now. Crying at her stupidity. Crying at her anger. Crying at her anger about her anger.

"Get up," said Dreck.

"Honestly. How rude can—"

Dreck smacked her with his pole, and she scrambled to her feet.

He pointed ahead. "Snow bear."

If she had thought Dreck was big, she was wrong. The animal that lumbered toward her was crunching on moose antlers like hard candy. It rose over five feet at the shoulders, and that was while it was on all fours. Its pelt was matted white fur, and its claws were as long as Blaze's hand.

"All right, monk. Weave your way out of this one," she said.

"Ember Mage turn."

"Right."

Blaze tried to light the spark, but the heat was slow in coming—she'd just squelched it. Now she needed time.

"Listen bear," she snapped. "You don't want to mess with me." She pointed a finger at it, like a hamster scolding a hound. "I've pretty much had my whole life screwed up and—"

The bear let loose a roar that knocked piles of snow off tree branches and flung streams of saliva toward her.

"Oh, it is on!" Blaze extended her hands. "Nobody drools on me. Go fire!"

Nothing.

This was not good.

Dreck exchanged a look of concern with Blaze. Then he heaved a great breath and gave a strange cacophonous cry, like an angry cow in the midst of a stampede.

The bear gave him a piece of its mind with an even louder roar.

Blaze's ears were now ringing nonstop. "Is that supposed to be helping or making it madder?" she asked.

Dreck began another round of horrendous noise making, even worse than the first.

The bear, which had been trying in vain to cover its ears with its paws, gave up and charged at Dreck.

If he was dinner, she would be desert.

In four lumbering strides the beast was in striking range.

The bear blocked out most of her view. Up close, it was far larger than she had imagined. Few times in her life had she felt so small—so helpless.

She was just a teenage girl. She couldn't even beat the local tavern brutes in an arm wrestle.

And this bear was going to tear Dreck apart. There had to be something she could do.

But no fire!

In pure desperation, Blaze leapt onto the bear's flank and flung her arms around its thick neck.

She failed to hold on. The bear turned wildly, bucking her off, and she managed to snag one ear as she swung under it.

Like a horse's head turned by a sharp bit, the bear's head veered downward. Blaze hadn't been *trying* to rip its ear off.

A heavy crack sounded as Blaze rolled clear. She looked up to see the giant beast slump forward and slide to a stop, its enormous tongue lolling out.

Dreck shouldered his staff. He'd dealt the knockout

blow. "Not sleep long. Good idea run."

"Bad grammar, but I agree," Blaze said. They didn't have time for anything else. Its hide was too thick.

The pair sprinted up an incline, then walked their way along a narrow ledge and descended into a deep ravine.

Blaze's terror at the encounter quickly turned to irritation. "Don't even tell me you didn't smell that thing, because even *I* could smell it."

"You actually listen. Not stop story," said Dreck.

"I was listening, so you didn't tell me that *thing* was about to eat us! Keep that up and your wandering days are going to stop at—what is it now—seven, eight?" She brandished her fist. "Or was this the path the Goddess chose for you: near death by bear breath?"

"Goddess not choose path. Monk choose own. Goddess fill with chances."

"You mean chances for death?"

"Chances for make friend," said Dreck.

That felt like a piece of ice slipping into her lung. How could Dreck think they were close? Occasional allies, maybe, but friends? She still wasn't even sure if she trusted him. The only reason she still traveled with him was so she knew where to go in this horrible, forbidden wasteland. In any other circumstance, she would be with anyone else, and Dreck? Well, Dreck would be alone.

Dreck surely noticed that she said nothing after his comment. But he was a monk after all. He couldn't hold a grudge. So, he had saved her life. His tribe—maybe even his father—had already taken her parents from her, and her village, and left her with a rage that had eventually gotten her thrown out of the Order of Ember and sent on a death-trap mission to these frozen slopes.

And then Princess Sapphire had not only forgiven them after all that, she had turned to them for help.

Dreck slowed as the trail flattened. "This meeting place." He approached the edge of the overlook, crawled down on his stomach and peered over. Blaze, curious despite her exhaustion, lay down on the bare rock and looked out over the wide canyon below.

Far down the canyon were the dim shapes of buildings. A city.

"What's that city near those frozen waterfalls?" Blaze asked. "Is that Dwarfholm Bastion?"

"Nope," Dreck said flatly. "You have a bad sense of direction. Do not travel alone. That is Foruk's Falls. Reach by treacherous canyon—twelve hours by foot. Full day by wagon."

Blaze seethed. Farther up the canyon was another cluster of dwellings dimmed by the smoky haze of campfires or fog. "So Dwarfholm Bastion is that black and red smudge down there?"

"Amazing," Dreck said. "You are wrong every time. That is Rimefrost war camp. Dwarfholm Bastion underground." He pointed to a line of peaks in the distance, beyond the ridge that defined the canyon. "See those black holes? Cavern entrances." He jabbed a finger at the settlements. "Orc war camp between dwarf cities. See the white smudges? Orc tents."

Blaze tilted her head, frowning. "I don't see any white smudges. I just see mounds of snow everywhere."

Dreck gave a low laugh. "You are dumb, but funny. You should do comedy."

"I am *not* funny. And I'm not dumb. You are just bad at explaining things." She followed the orc, glaring at his back.

"Maybe," the orc said. "But my chief never tell me so. Perhaps he send message soon."

Rav was gone. Blaze had forgotten about that.

"So, we're basically waiting for Princess Sapphire. What's the plan once she gets here?"

"Dreck not know." He rolled back his shoulders. The orc was impossible to read. Was he nervous? Glad? Confident? Eager?

"What time is she supposed to be here?" Blaze said. Hiking, she could handle. Sitting still and waiting to get found, not at all.

Dreck did not answer. He inhaled slowly, for what seemed like an entire minute.

Good grief, how large are his lungs?

"Orcs coming."

"Orcs. Which orcs? Crook-Eye Orcs—the orcs bringing

Princess Sapphire?"

Dreck held out his hand for silence.

The low sun cast long shadows across the snow, like daggers and arrows in flight.

Twilight.

Blaze let her anxiety build, drawing it to a point within her. If it was the enemy, they weren't going to get a friendly welcome from her. There weren't many human teenagers with the stamina to hike all day in the Frostbyte Reach and still be ready for action.

There was probably only one.

Blaze was nearly acclimated to the altitude, had eaten decent food, and still had plenty of energy to channel her inner fire. She was ticked off at the Order of Ember, at the Rimefrost Orcs, at the bear, at Dreck's story about Princess Sapphire releasing the Crook-Eye tribe—at nearly everything. The slightest incident would put her over the edge. She regulated her breathing, staying just below the ignition point. She couldn't afford to summon the fire too early and flame out before the danger arrived. The incident with the bear had nearly cost both of them their lives.

She stretched her fingers, listening for the sounds of approaching feet.

Like Dreck, these orcs knew how to move in silence. He sniffed again and made a fist, the bone spurs on his knuckles rising.

The Kings Summons

That's not good.

There was a slight flash of blue on the edge of the wood. Strange. Blaze thought she recognized it, then it was gone.

Shadows shifted in a cluster of quaking aspens to their right. The trees trembled and three full-sized orcs stepped into the clearing.

Blaze had forgotten how much larger they were than Dreck. He was nearly as tall as them, but they were almost twice as wide, and surely twice as strong.

Blaze could make out their tusks jutting up from their jaw. But the patterns on their faces—the tell-tale tattoos—were still in shadow.

"Hail, orc-cousins," said Dreck. He held up a hand in greeting.

The three orcs did not reply but took two steps closer.

"Dreck, what is going on? Where is the pr—"

A small gesture from Dreck's hand cut her off.

This is not good.

She could now see two of the orcs well enough to make out a curling tattoo over their eyes. Crook-Eyes. The one in the center—the largest—wore a helmet. It was lined by snow bear fur.

Rimefrost Orc.

She felt the spark inside grow. She nursed it.

The two Crook-Eyes stepped back from the helmeted orc.

So, if the Rimefrost Orc wasn't their prisoner. That meant . . .

I am.

"Goddess-loving, Dreck," said the orc on the right. "Better you not come here."

"You said we were going to meet your—what is going on, Dreck?" Blaze whispered.

"Where my father?" Dreck said, his voice and his staff steady.

"With the rest," said the Rimefrost Orc, "of the unworthy."

Blaze desperately wanted to ask if Princess Sapphire was among their captives, but she couldn't risk it. There was a chance they didn't know she was here. She had to find out what she could before she gave anything away.

"What unworthy?" Blaze said. "How many?"

"All who follow Goddess," said the orc on the left. "Human." He glowered at Blaze.

Dreck's face made the first expression Blaze could recognize. He was hurt by what this orc had said. He knew him.

"So, you found out we were coming and came to capture us?" Blaze said.

"Urkit tell Crook-Eye to send message." The Rimefrost Orc beat his chest with his fist. "Urkit find true orcs—kill the rest."

"No," Dreck said.

The Kings Summons

"First you see new orc power. Then you die."

That's it. Flame on.

Blaze lit her inner fire. The world flashed suddenly red, as if the sun had set. This time, she did not light fire on her hands; she wouldn't hurl fireballs, but massed all of it within herself, building a volcano on the verge of eruption. Any trace of cold disappeared. The snow beneath her feet began to soften.

"I hate to break it to you," Blaze said. "But three of you versus an Ember Mage—it's not going to go well. And trust me when I tell you there is no more painful way to die than by fire."

The orcs laughed. More shadows shifted behind them. From behind every tree in the wood massive orcs stalked forward, some with clubs, others with hammers, others with bows as thick as Blaze's thigh, or swords large enough to fell a tree. At least a dozen of them were armed with the same rune-marked shields that had repelled her fire earlier. She was outmatched.

She looked over her shoulder. There were even more behind her.

"Dreck—how could this happen? Was this a trap— did you know about this?"

"Dreck not know. Dreck always suspect orc. Darkness here make friends enemies." He looked at the orc on the left who remained just as unreadable.

"What are we going to do?" said Blaze. "We can't just

surrender."

Dreck held out his staff in both hands and let it fall. "Dreck not fight."

"Oh, come on." Blaze lit her hands. "Fine. I'll do this myself." Blaze hurled two fireballs before a net of cold metal wrapped around her from behind. As soon as the cables of woven wire touched her, the fire within shorted out.

The spark!

What had taken over a minute to build up was gone in a flash. Blaze struggled in the net. There were flashing red amulets and shaman's tokens woven into the wire. They pulsed as her fire passed through the net and back into the ground, flash-evaporating a circle of snow all around her.

Blaze tried to throw the net off, but the short circuit had left her dizzy. She gave one pull on the net and fell to the ground, exhausted and drained. The snow sizzled beneath her.

The Rimefrost Orcs stomped and whooped, bellowing terrible cries as they bound the net around her and slung her to a pole. She could not see Dreck.

Had they bound him as well? Had they let him go?

Please no. Don't let this happen.

The orc troop descended the steep canyon, hauling Blaze on the pole. All too soon, the bonfires of the war camp flickered on all sides.

Horns blared out as they approached. The orcs

dropped her onto the hard-packed snow. The cold metal net bit into her skin. She was already shivering with ember afterchill. She couldn't stop.

The ground shook, and Blaze looked up. "No!" she cried.

Bound to the ground with a tangled array of cables and nets was an enormous figure lying on its back. Glowing red lines appeared in a crisscross pattern where the cables bit into its ice-like, snowy-white skin.

The orcs had captured the jotnar.

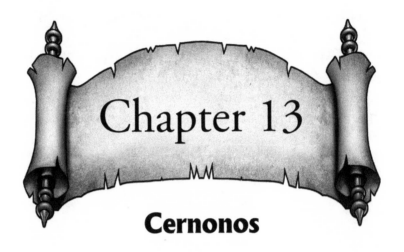

Chapter 13

Cernonos

The great jotnar was surrounded by no less than two hundred orcs, all armed with long-bladed spears. The jotnar moved its leg, and immediately a dozen guards jabbed their weapons at it. The jotnar convulsed as the dark magic of the blades flowed into it, assaulting its very nature.

Blaze knew the feeling.

She was withering. She didn't know how much longer she could survive with the cold net wrapped around her, cutting into her. Its magic cables were draining every degree of heat she could summon.

And then the creature stepped from behind the jotnar. Blaze stared in horror.

She had heard of chimera before—half-man, half-animal demons. Long, obsidian black horns grew upward out of his skull. Ornate metal ringed his horns halfway down their length. His chest was shielded by metal armor plates, and his shoulders were covered in brown matted fur. His hands were massive, nearly the size of Blaze's entire torso. His feet and legs resembled the hind legs of a goat.

His face was just human enough to make the entire repulsive creature look intelligent. The most disturbing thing was his eyes. They glowed bright blue, stark and terrifying against the dark, wintry night.

Rune tattoos covered his armor, powerful spells that would repel harm and grant him supernatural strength in battle.

"Cernonos." An orc captain took a knee in front of the demon. "We have the Ember Mage that attacked Hetsa, and last of the Crook-Eye traitors."

Dreck is alive.

"Good. The sacrifice of these prisoners will only bind the Iron Collar stronger," said Cernonos. His voice dripped with malice.

Whatever hope Blaze had clung to was draining fast.

"Our Midnight Queen requires an army of dark jotnar. This will be but the first."

The Midnight Queen. That was the same name that the ice kobolds had mentioned when Blaze first arrived in the Frostbyte Reach. Was that some new sorceress in league with the Dark Consul? Could that be the one who was behind the expansion of dark influence spreading through Crystalia?

Crystalians had turned to darkness before: the Consul, the Usurper King . . . and now perhaps there were some turning to this Midnight Queen.

And how powerful was this being if monsters like Cernonos served her?

"The Frostbyte Reach will soon fall to our might," said Cernonos. "Then all of Crystalia—and all too easy. The power to destroy them was here all along, waiting for us to claim it. Take the prisoners to the rune marks! Their strength will be mine to command. The binding curse will be unbreakable!"

Two Rimefrost Orcs seized Blaze tightly around the arms and dragged her across the ice. They dropped her into a triangle drawn on the ice with a black substance that looked like pitch.

The jotnar was less than four yards away. To her right and left, four Crook-Eye Orcs bound by thick cords were each shoved into their own triangles. Lines of pitch linked the triangles together in a semicircle around the jotnar.

The Kings Summons

This can't be happening, Blaze thought, as she trembled with shivers. Orcs behind her laughed. When the last triangle was filled, the orc captain gave a guttural cry and the soldiers guarding the jotnar stepped back.

Six orcs pushed an enormous wooden wagon toward the jotnar. They pulled back a tarp covering the wagon, and Cernonos lifted out a black wrought iron hoop—the Iron Collar.

The Iron Collar that Dreck, the traitor, had given to them.

In its center was set what looked like a shining black diamond—the black zirconia.

So it *was* true. She'd confronted Dreck about it, and he'd refused to tell her. The orc with the raven in Hetsa seeking the black zirconia *had* been Dreck.

How long had Dreck been planning this? Blaze felt sick to her stomach. She'd been right not to trust him.

A shadow flickered on Blaze's right and with it a flash of something blue. Blaze had seen that light before, bright against a flame. Could it be?

But the light was gone just as quickly as it had come.

Cernonos raised the heavy collar with his bare hands. His hands glowed red, and the runes carved into the metal glowed. As they did, the Iron Collar expanded and grew, nearly doubling in circumference.

Cernonos gripped it with both hands at the top of the hoop and unlatched it. The collar bent on a hidden hinge, and Cernonos clamped it shut over the neck of the captive jotnar.

Orcs scrambled to latch a chain to the collar behind the nape of the jotnar's neck, then pulled.

The jotnar struggled against its bonds, moaning a soft, sad cry.

Cernonos stepped forward and raised his arms, speaking in an arcane tongue.

The red-glowing cords that crisscrossed the jotnar's bound body pulsed with energy. The ice giant gave a great roar that shook the canyon walls, and suddenly the lines of pitch that formed each triangle lit up with red fire. The flames were so close, they warmed the skin on Blaze's cheeks.

She stretched her hand as far as she could through the metal net's weave. If she could just reach it, she could use it to charge up. The burning pitch was just beyond her fingertips.

Suddenly the chords of her net loosened behind her, then something unseen shoved her from behind. She scraped forward just a few inches. It was enough. Blaze thrust her fist into the burning flame. It enveloped her hand.

Warmth surged into Blaze.

"On my signal, not before." The words came to her as if from thin air. Blaze knew that voice. Blaze stifled a cry of excitement. There was hope in that voice.

The Kings Summons

She siphoned more heat from the glowing flames. The scene turned a reddish hue.

Cernonos roared the words of his spell ever louder, and again the red lines pulsed. The jotnar cried out in pain and terror.

Blaze saw the same flash of faint blue light in front of her. This time it grew, glowing and forming into the figure of a young woman, fully clad in shining, silvery-blue armor, a broadsword with blade edges glowing blue in each hand, her blue hair flowing out from beneath a narrow-slotted battle helmet that shielded all but her fierce blue eyes.

It was just as she had looked on the day Blaze had first met her.

Princess Sapphire.

Only now the princess was so much stronger and more magnificent.

"You're here," whispered Blaze. This was exactly what Blaze had come for. Except that Princess Sapphire had found Blaze instead. A surge of joy welled up inside Blaze, and for a split second, Blaze's vision faded from red to white.

Princess Sapphire was alive. And Blaze had forgotten just how gloriously, splendidly awesome the princess was.

Princess Sapphire made her move. Her blurred figure, like a moving curtain, raced along the edges of the triangle. Her two blue-edged swords, one afire, flashed like lightning as she severed binding cords and cut through the boundaries of the carefully crafted rune marks.

Cernonos roared his spell, his chant sending a surge of heat into the triangles. "You!" he cried.

"I'll take that," Blaze said. Siphoning the heat of Cernonos's spell out of the triangle, Blaze filled to capacity in an instant. She threw her arms outward, obliterating the metal net in a blast of fire. Fragments of molten cable whipped into the orc soldiers surrounding the ceremony.

Now it was time to play.

Blaze leapt from her triangle. She was immediately thrown back into its center by an unseen force.

The triangle's binding spell held her captive. *I can fix that.*

Blaze sent out lines of fire to the neighboring triangles and siphoned their fire into her as well. The Crook-Eye Orcs within were momentarily free.

Drawing in the rest of the fire from her triangle rune mark, she extinguished the burning pitch.

Soldiers with lances surged forward to stop the captives from escaping. Blaze had to stop them before their cursed lances reached the unarmed Crook-Eyes.

"Fire Wave!" Blaze sent an entire company of orcs scrambling for their lives as tongues of flame jetted out from Blaze's fingers. She turned and scorched the line between attackers and captives on the other side.

Claiming the fallen lances, Crook-Eye Orcs began

slashing at the jotnar's bands to free it. An entire company of Crook-Eyes charged forward, leaving the Rimefrost Orcs and coming to their tribesmen's aid, hacking at the jotnar's bands as well.

The Crook-Eyes were on Princess Sapphire's side! It had all been a trick. The Crook-Eye Orcs must have allowed some of their number to infiltrate the Rimefrost camp and betray their tribesmen.

Now all fought side-by-side to free the great ice giant. But the jotnar didn't move.

Blaze turned to see Cernonos holding its collar with one hand, chanting a spell. Red fire coursed from the runes on his armor, running down his hands and into the metal. The black diamond shone and flashed as the magic danced through it.

Princess Sapphire raced around the foot of the giant toward Blaze, the last of the glowing blue light fading behind her. She was joined by a group of recently-freed Crook-Eye Orcs, who came charging around from the other side of the giant.

Another burst of red magic coursed through the runes on the Iron Collar. The jotnar's arms flung outward.

Princess Sapphire leapt backward, dodging. A few of the Crook-Eye Orcs weren't so lucky.

"Cernonos is using his own strength to seal the spell!" the princess cried. "It's too late—retreat!"

Blaze leapt to her feet. This was her chance. "No. I can

159

stop him," she said.

Princess Sapphire turned, her fiery blue eyes staring directly at Blaze. "No. I said *retreat*, soldier," said the princess. "That is an order."

Blaze smoldered inside. She was fully charged up. She could do this. Blaze could show Princess Sapphire that she could fight alongside her. She could win.

She summoned a fireball and hurled it with dead-eye accuracy, right into the black diamond in the center of the Iron Collar.

Cernonos screamed and recoiled, his hands all aflame. Blaze concentrated her blast, holding it until the fireball turned into a column of flame. She focused that column into a narrow blast on the black diamond. The jotnar screamed.

"No!" Princess Sapphire cried.

Princess Sapphire smashed into Blaze, knocking her aside and breaking Blaze's column of flame.

But it was too late. The black diamond had melted in the collar.

Melted? That's impossible. Ember fire was hot enough to turn molten rock into lava, but never melt a diamond.

"Black zirconia!" roared Cernonos. "A hidden dampening spell! The Crook-Eyes betrayed us!"

"He knows," grunted a huge orc that looked strangely familiar—a larger version of Dreck. "It's all for naught!"

Rimefrost Orc soldiers surrounded Cernonos and

interlocked fire-repelling shields in a circle around him.

"What have you done?" Princess Sapphire said, her blue eyes staring into Blaze's. "That was our last chance to sabotage the spell."

"I didn't know!" Blaze gasped. She didn't quite understand what she had done, but a cold, sinking feeling dropped into her stomach.

With a roar of anger, Cernonos jammed a clawed thumb into what was left of the melted black zirconia and tore it from the collar. He pressed his palm to the broken fitting. The collar began to glow.

"Don't let him seal the spell!" Princess Sapphire cried.

The princess raised her flaming broadsword high, rallying the soldiers. She charged forward, ready to throw herself into the heart of the battle. But suddenly there was a noise like a blanket being thrown over the world, damping all noise. For a moment, Blaze again seemed to hang in a space apart from her surroundings.

A blast of sparks erupted from the giant's collar where Cernonos held it between his hands. A crack of thunder boomed over the chaos of the battle.

"No!" Blaze cried.

"Fall back!" Princess Sapphire ordered.

A wave of retreating Crook-Eye Orcs pushed Blaze back from the jotnar. Blaze watched in horror as the jotnar's eyes opened.

Red.

"Run!" said a voice. Blaze felt herself yanked up under the arm of an orc wearing a long robe.

"Dreck?" Blaze asked.

"Mmmph," Dreck grunted in reply.

"To Foruk's Falls," Princess Sapphire cried, sprinting— in full armor. She kept pace with even the largest orcs. "The city has only a few guards now. We must evacuate the dwarves and freyjan before the jotnar reaches the city."

Four huge snow bears with two Rimefrost Orc riders each charged between the trees, closing in from either side ahead of the Crook-Eye tribe.

"Snow bear," grunted a nearby Crook-Eye. "Orc up!" The Crook-Eyes were quick. One by one, the Crook-Eye Orcs joined hands and launched their tribesmen into the air. The airborne Crook-Eye Orcs smashed into the snow bear riders, knocking them off their mounts and taking their places.

The Crook-Eyes took the reins of the muzzled snow bears, slowing them enough for a half-dozen more Crook-Eye Orcs to climb aboard each gigantic bear. Dreck tossed Blaze onto the last snow bear and hauled himself up its fur.

"Ride!" Princess Sapphire called, standing atop the lead bear. Her blue-tinged sword flashed briefly, and the snow bears charged out of the Rimefrost camp as a great moan rose up from behind them.

It was a sad sound, like the north wind itself dying.

The Kings Summons

The jotnar had fallen to darkness.

Blaze clung to the matted white fur as the great bear lumbered down the canyon toward Foruk's Falls. She shivered violently. She spent every last spark. Dreck wrapped Blaze in his arms and held her while the afterchill claimed her once again. She wanted to struggle. She wanted to push him away. But she was just too tired.

They had failed. The Frostbyte Reach was doomed.

Chapter 14

The Torch Road

The snows bears slowed to a halt after a few miles.

"Looks like they're out of steam," said Princess Sapphire. "No matter. This is our stop." She called to a Crook-Eye shaman. "Orktag, I do not want to see these creatures in battle again, especially sneaking up behind us—knock them out."

The orcs dismounted, and Blaze leapt down, glad to be off the back of something that considered her a modest snack. They were lazy creatures anyway. The snow bears should have taken them at least as far as Foruk's Falls.

Orktag the shaman drew out a ball on a cord and swung it in turn at the noses of the bears, releasing a puff of sparkling dust. A moment later, each bear collapsed in a heap.

Princess Sapphire held her sword aloft, a bright blue glow emanating from the gem in its hilt. Her eyes were a deep, almost ocean blue, piercing and discerning. She looked, for all the world, like she could command the whole kingdom at a word. She peered into the deep woods, as if searching for something.

"How long will they stay down?" she turned and asked.

"They're in their winter sleep now," said the shaman. "I broke the Rimefrost spell that kept them awake."

"Hibernation—excellent," said Princess Sapphire. She turned aside and into the woods, leaving the trail behind. "This way."

Blaze poked Dreck in his rock-hard abs. "See, that's how it's done. You need to get some of that shaman powder, Dreck. Then you might actually be useful."

"Dreck have allergies to shaman magic," said Dreck.

"Oh."

"Kidding."

Blaze looked up to see Dreck making his horrible, open-faced, smile-gape thing. It was ridiculous. She wasn't going to give him the satisfaction of laughing at his jokes.

"Wipe that smile off your face, orc. You look like you swallowed a dragon egg."

Blaze looked around to see if anyone was watching. "Come on, let's keep up with the princess. We don't want to be here when Cernonos shows up with the dark jotnar. They can't be far behind."

For a moment, Blaze's conscience pricked her. *Shouldn't I be grateful?* He had saved her from freezing. She pushed the thought from her mind. Hadn't Dreck been the one to help Cernonos? He *had* been part of some grander plan. But did that mean she could trust him? She still wasn't sure.

Between the leafless branches of the aspens, Princess Sapphire's dark blue hair waved in the breeze, the tips wrapped in silvery bands as she hurried into the forest. Her armor shone in the faint light of her blue-glowing gem, glittering as though reinforced with hundreds of tiny diamonds. She carried on her back a large shield bearing the royal crest. It looked the same as the one she had lost in the fire. Perhaps she had retrieved it or had it remade.

Blaze jogged in Dreck's oversized footprints, leaving the trail behind and weaving into a wintery wood dense with underbrush.

"This is crazy," Blaze said between heavy breaths, not loud enough to question the princess's authority. "We're going to get lost in here."

As if in answer, the company of jogging orcs parted,

and Princess Sapphire moved next to Blaze. "Ember Mage! I see you have joined our company," Princess Sapphire said. There was disapproval in her voice. She glanced at Blaze's empty hands. "I am sorry to see you have lost your staff. That would have been useful."

Did she know? Either way, the comment stung. Blaze pushed back the start of a tear. "Uh, yeah. It's real sad."

After all these years of idolizing Princess Sapphire, the princess talked to her like this? Did she know that she was everything Blaze wanted to be? Did she know that Blaze had come all the way to the bitter cold of the Frostbyte Reach just to find her? Blaze had risked everything to find her.

Worse yet, Blaze had made a grave mistake in Princess Sapphire's eyes when Blaze had melted the black diamond. Blaze hadn't meant to. She had just been trying to save the jotnar.

Princess Sapphire didn't seem to notice Blaze's discomfort. She looked to Dreck. "Our carefully laid plans will have to change course."

Dreck grunted in agreement. "Yes, Your Majesty."

How well did Dreck know the princess? Clearly, they had made plans together. All this time Blaze had been trying to protect Princess Sapphire by not telling Dreck that she was here. But Dreck knew anyway. Apparently there was a lot more Dreck knew that he wasn't telling *her*.

"And where did you find this tagalong?" Princess

Sapphire asked. She glanced toward Blaze. That was *not* what Blaze wanted to be called. She was so much more than that, wasn't she?

"He was helping me," said Blaze.

"Oh," said Princess Sapphire, "To do what?"

"He was helping me find you," muttered Blaze. Then she added quickly, "Your Majesty."

Princess Sapphire gave a quizzical expression. "Why were you looking for me?"

"Ah," Blaze said, failing to think of a sophisticated way to explain it. "Your father was worried about you. Said he hadn't heard from you in weeks. He sent me to discover if you'd been waylaid or kidnapped or . . . you know. Killed."

"Killed?" Princess Sapphire said, her voice serious. "Yes, that sounds like father. I am sorry I made him worry, but my task here is important." Her eyes became distant. "We were so close to saving that jotnar," she said in a whisper, not loud enough for the others to hear.

"I . . ." Blaze said. She couldn't find the words. She wanted to apologize for melting the black diamond, but she wasn't quite sure how to say it. "I didn't mean to . . ."

Princess Sapphire cut her off. "What's done is done," she said. "We'd been planning that for months. When we found out that the Iron Collar was on its way to Cernonos, we intercepted it. Cernonos wasn't going to stop until he had it. So we gave it to him but on our terms. Modified, sabotaged, and with only one small problem—it didn't quite work. The black diamond acted as a suppressant. It actually blocked the runes from working. It's delicate magic. It would have taken him weeks, maybe even months to figure out why it had failed. And that would have bought us precious time."

Blaze looked down at the snow. "So you knew Dreck was going to give it to him."

"Knew?" said Princess Sapphire. "The Iron Collar. The black diamond. That was all part of the plan. Dreck had been working for me from the very start."

Blaze smoldered inside, but this time, it was less from hurt than embarrassment. How could she have been so wrong about so many things? She thought she saw Dreck looking at her from the corner of her vision. She couldn't meet his eyes. Not now.

"And now we need new plans," said Princess Sapphire. "To deal with an entirely new set of circumstances."

Princess Sapphire looked at Blaze again. Her majestic features seemed to soften. "So, King Worrywart sent an Ember Mage to the Frostbyte Reach." She shook her head. "Typical."

Then she added with a slight smile. "Dad," she said to herself.

"Speaking of staffs, Dreck—where is yours?" Princess Sapphire asked.

"Taken by the Rimefrost Orcs," said Dreck. He lifted a heavy bow. "Took this instead."

"Good," said Princess Sapphire. "Now where *is* that entrance?"

Princess Sapphire kicked at a large rock, and a levered hatchway opened up and inward, revealing a low-ceilinged passage. It was lit by torches mounted on the walls.

A blast of warm air wrapped around Blaze and warmed her face. "Dwarf tunnel—brilliant!" said Blaze. At least they'd be sheltered from the wind in there, and it would be nice to be out of the snow for once.

"Not just any dwarf tunnel. This is a branch of the Torch Road. Everyone below!" commanded Princess Sapphire. "Cernonos will be right behind us. Our best hope is that he doesn't find this entrance."

Blaze went first, carefully ducking down below the surface. The Crook-Eye Orcs squeezed in behind her.

The walls were evenly carved, and the floor was paved with perfectly cut, flat stones. The craftsmanship was incredible. There wasn't a hint of imperfection in the floor, except where a pair of metal rails ran along the floor into a branch of the tunnel. So this portion had been a mine once. It branched into three tunnels.

Just in front of Blaze was a large, overturned, round-bottomed bucket on wheels—a mine car. It trembled slightly.

It wasn't empty.

Princess Sapphire sniffed. "I thought I smelled mead," she said. She struck the side of the metal mine car like a gong. It rang out, echoing down the passage. Two napping dwarfs snorted in unison and leapt to their feet, facing opposite directions, their fists raised to fight.

"Intruders!" called one.

"I'll break their necks!" bellowed the other.

One wore a brass belt buckle almost the size of a dinner plate that read "BORT" in bold letters, and the other wore an equally ostentatious buckle with the word "TORT" written on it. Each dwarf had an enormous ax strapped to his back and looked about as thick around as an orc, minus a significant amount of height.

Princess Sapphire stood unflinching, looking them over. "Ah, the Thunder Twins," she said. "Famous for your antics, exploits, and perhaps most of all, your mischief."

The two heavyset dwarves turned to face her. They dropped their jaws. "You're . . ." muttered one.

"Yes, I'm Princess Sapphire," she said. "An honor to meet you both. We need to use this branch of the Torch Road to get to Foruk's Falls. There is a secret entrance into the city. Can you lead us there?"

They grinned toothy grins.

"Right this way," said Bort, pointing left.

"You mean this way," said Tort, pointing right.

Princess Sapphire glared at them. "I'll take that as a yes," she said.

The twins nodded at each other. Despite their long beards, they couldn't have been more than adolescents.

Their dark, beady eyes sparkled with life.

"Let's go that way," they both said, pointing down a middle passage.

They scrambled down the passage. Princess Sapphire marched after them. Blaze and the orcs followed close behind.

The torches embedded every few feet into the rock gave off a warm, yellow glow that filled the whole tunnel. It was brighter than any tavern lit by a blazing hearth and lamplight. An occasional purple or green gem embedded in the rock flashed as they passed.

"What news can you give me of King Holm Everbright?" Princess Sapphire asked.

"Dad—same as always. We knew something was happening here in the Reach. We've been watching the orcs move. So, Dad told us to stay put," said Bort.

"May as well have ordered us to come," said Tort. "We thought armies would be here days ago to free Foruk's Falls. What took you so long?"

"Our battle did not go well," Princess Sapphire said. "A jotnar is under Cernonos's control. We have only a matter of hours to free Foruk's Falls and regroup before that monster lays waste to the entire valley."

Veins popped up on the twins' foreheads like trails from a burrowing mole on a lawn. Their jaws clenched in anger, and Tort shook like he was going to explode. "How dare they!" Bort cried through bits of spittle that escaped through his mustache.

"We planted a false gem in the Iron Collar to sabotage their plan," said Princess Sapphire. "It would have left a critical weakness in the Iron Collar used to control the jotnar."

"What happened?" Bort demanded.

"It . . . was discovered," Princess Sapphire said, without looking at Blaze.

"We could've—" started Blaze.

"No you could not," Princess Sapphire cut her off. Suddenly Blaze felt small and helpless.

"What we need now is a plan," said Princess Sapphire.

Bort gave a vicious grin. "To free Foruk's Falls? No problem." He scratched his beard for a moment, then looked at Tort. "Are you thinking what I'm thinking?"

Tort rubbed his hands together. "Ever capture a snow fort from your friends?"

Princess Sapphire shook her head.

"The key is to lure them out and then claim it for yourself," said Tort.

"I see. So who will lure them out while we wait to claim the city?" asked Princess Sapphire.

Tort pointed at Blaze. "I vote her."

"Seconded," echoed the other twin.

Me? What was she going to do? "Twins only get one vote," she said.

"Well it certainly won't be one of them," said Princess

173

Sapphire, pointing to the brawny Crook-Eyes. "Thirded," she said. "I'm not even sure that's a word."

"I once heard Gork say it," Tort droned. "So, it's a word."

The princess inclined her head. "Gork is their older brother. He's next in line for the throne."

"The runt," said the twins in unison.

Princess Sapphire turned to Blaze. "Here's your chance, Ember Mage. What is your plan to lure the orcs out of the city?"

Blaze's mind drained of thought. With a princess and two dwarf princes staring at her, the pressure was on. She drew her hood close to hide her embarrassment.

"Well, we need to make them think that if they wait to attack, things will only get worse—I can cast a few fire spells to make it convincing. But we need them to bring their entire garrison outside the walls. How can I—"

Tort interrupted her. "Meanwhile, we'll sneak in through a secret tunnel and lock the gates behind them."

"Anyone left inside," Bort chuckled to himself, "gets to deal with me."

"And me!" cried Tort.

"You only get a third of them, Tort, since you get to lock the gates. I get two thirds."

"I don't want to lock the gates. You lock the gates. I get two thirds."

"Boys!" Princess Sapphire snapped. "That's quite

enough. You will both lock the gates, and I get anyone left."

"Pulling rank . . ." Bort grumbled.

Despite the dwarf's natural overconfidence, the whole venture hinged on Blaze being able to come up with a distraction so grand the orcs would be forced to attack immediately.

So give them what they want.

"Princess, we need to switch clothes," said Blaze.

"I see," Princess Sapphire said, her eyes narrowing at Blaze.

The Thunder Twins looked back and forth at both of them.

"We have a dwarvish army at the end of this tunnel," said Bort. "They've been watching Foruk's Falls, lying in wait for King Holm Everbright to send orders from Dwarfholm Bastion."

Princess Sapphire brightened. "How many soldiers?"

Bort started counting on his fingers. When he used them up, he started using Tort's. "Can you take off my boots? I'm not done counting yet."

"No!" Princess Sapphire exclaimed. Out of the side of her mouth she whispered. "Never take off a dwarf's boots in an enclosed space."

She gave a nod of approval. "I think that will be enough if what the Ember Mage has in mind is as good as I think it is."

175

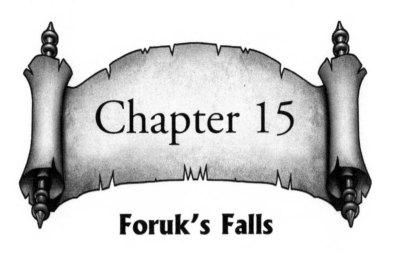

Chapter 15

Foruk's Falls

"It's not going to be enough."

Blaze stood beside Princess Sapphire, who bit her lip as she surveyed the group.

The dwarf soldiers had gathered in the secret tunnel beneath the ancient city of Foruk's Falls. They weren't nearly as beefy as Bort or Tort. The Thunder Twins, despite their dwarvish stature, outweighed most full-grown men. The dwarf soldiers were a head shorter than Blaze, who was already done with most of her growth. They were well disciplined, keeping to absolute silence before the assault, and their mail and armor was in good condition. But there just weren't enough of them.

Only a few dozen feet overhead was an entire city being held hostage. "The scouts report that things are bad up there. The people can't hold out much longer under orc rule," said Princess Sapphire.

"You don't have any more of that concealment potion you used earlier, do you?" Blaze asked.

"Not hardly. One bottle is worth a small fiefdom. And you—any potions?" said Princess Sapphire.

"Used up my Fire Water on a company of kobolds. It was a good thing the quartermaster at Crystalia Castle put some in the top of my pack."

"He did the same trick to me," Princess Sapphire said. "I wouldn't have taken the Essence of Glass from the Castle if I had known it was in there. It might have been our last bottle."

For all the danger that awaited them outside, Princess Sapphire did not seem on edge. Clearly, she had been in a major battle before and knew how to keep her nerves.

Blaze felt like a nervous wreck. "I'll, um, take the shaman, and another six of the elder Crook-Eyes," Blaze said. After a moment's pause, she sighed. *He's the only one I know.* "And I'll take Dreck. You can take the younger warriors. They'll be more useful in the battle."

"Very well," Princess Sapphire said. "Good luck to

you." She handed Blaze her second, smaller sword. The one that didn't flame. Blaze would have had a hard time wielding the larger, first sword convincingly. "And don't mess this up."

Blaze gulped. Here was her hero, giving her an impossible mission, even though Blaze had ruined their plan to save the jotnar. No pressure.

Princess Sapphire raised her sword. "The people of Foruk's Falls are slaves to the army of the Dark Consul," she said, her voice echoing down the tunnel. "Their food feeds the orc overlords. Their homes and taverns have been turned to barracks. The citizens are treated like beasts of burden. But today, we free them!"

The dwarves banged their axes against their shields just once, then fell silent again.

It was time. Blaze was going out in front of an entire orc garrison dressed as one of the five most wanted people on the Dark Consul's list—the crown Princess Sapphire.

"Tell plan," Dreck said. He was surrounded by several of his tribesmen, each aged beyond their prime. Strong, but not as powerful in battle as the warriors that would go with Princess Sapphire.

"We'll talk on the way," Blaze said. She led the way up a side tunnel, using the gem in the sword hilt to light the way. It seemed to fill all of the dark corners with its light.

"Princess Sapphire said the tunnel bought us several hours on Cernonos's army, if not an entire day," Blaze said.

The Kings Summons

"But they will be here soon. Our best chance is to defeat the army at Foruk's Falls before they combine forces with Cernonos's army."

"So how?" said an orc.

"We will try to draw the orcs out of the city, while Princess Sapphire and the dwarves capture the fortifications and free the dwarf soldiers being held captive.

"Divide enemy. Join allies," Dreck said. "Good plan."

"It's our best hope of surviving," said Blaze. She was trying to act confident. Now that Princess Sapphire was separated from them, Blaze had to at least pretend she knew what she was doing.

She still had no idea though how the fortifications at Foruk's Falls could withstand an assault from an ice giant. *Better to have some defense over none.*

"Now listen carefully," Blaze said. "This is what we humans call 'a charade.'"

Minutes later, Blaze and her orc entourage emerged from the hidden tunnel exit less than a quarter mile from the city gates.

For the first time, Blaze was able to see the city up close. Built at the base of a huge granite mountain, Foruk's Falls was protected by a half-circle wall protruding from the rock on either side. The homes, taverns, estates, and shops were tucked safely inside the semi-circle wall. Perhaps the most striking feature of all, the landmark that had given the city its name, was the enormous frozen waterfall that had fallen from the mountainside into the center of the city. It looked like a giant stalagmite, a column of sparkling blue and white ice that must have weighed as much as a small mountain.

Closer to Blaze, the evergreens on either side of the canyon road were thick enough to provide cover. Her palms were already sweating inside Princess Sapphire's gauntlets despite the midnight chill.

Stars overhead winked their various approvals and doubts about the forthcoming battle. Beside her, the Crook-Eye Orcs waited motionless.

Perfect.

With a prayer to the Goddess, Blaze raised her arm and gave the signal.

Princess Sapphire would be in position by now. She had to be.

Dreck draped his arm over the Crook-Eye Orc shaman Orktag. The two of them trudged through the snow toward the city gates, Dreck dragging his leg as if it were hurt and leaning most of his weight on Orktag.

Orktag gave an orc signal, a barking grunt that sounded through the forest like a moose call.

It was a cry of warning.

The shaman repeated the call, and the orcs near Blaze began adding their calls to his, like a chorus of wolves

The Kings Summons

baying at the moon.

It was a terrifying sound, even though Blaze knew they were on her side.

She let the touch of fear ignite her spark. The familiar rush of volcanic heat flooded through her.

Guards atop the city wall brought torches to the front gate as Dreck and Orktag arrived beneath it.

"We spotted Princess Sapphire in the woods," said Orktag hurriedly, out of breath. He spoke so loudly that the still night air carried his voice all the way to Blaze in the woods. "She opened some kind of portal to Crystalia Castle. She intends to bring the king's guards here, through the portal."

Orcs barked the information over the walls. There was a rustling on the other side and soon the main gate opened to reveal three hulking Rimefrost Orc captains.

"Princess here!" repeated the largest Rimefrost captain. He motioned to the woods. "Right outside the gate. We take her now! Then we'll follow the portal to Crystalia Castle—we'll drink the blood of King Jasper! Battle and glory!"

The orcs hooted and pounded their armor.

"But the princess has powerful magic!" grunted Orktag. "She's used her magic on this one. His leg is like stone."

Dreck groaned, dragging his leg behind him.

"Bring all the warriors!" the Rimefrost Orc captain commanded. "The princess is strong and crafty."

The remaining Crook-Eye Orcs fled from their hiding places in the woods, barking warning cries and charging toward the city walls, as if they were filled with terror.

Blaze ran behind them. She pulled one gauntlet off and let it dangle by its tie to her wrist. It did feel good to be dressed as Princess Sapphire, even if it did mean that she was a target.

She sent a few fireballs in their direction, spreading her fingers to dissipate the fireballs before they harmlessly hit the Crook-Eye Orcs. It would add the perfect touch to the illusion that they were under attack.

She neared the edge of the wood before the open field at the foot of the city gates. There she stopped and, with her one ungauntleted hand, focused her fire into a glowing pillar. If she concentrated enough, she could change the fire's hue. She focused, sending just the right twist, and turned the pillar a shining white. Then she shaped it, turning it until it swirled into a concentrated sphere. The huge, white glowing orb looked just like the portals back in King Jasper's chambers at Crystalia Castle: direct access points to the inner castle and the king himself.

Then she stepped out of the woods into the moonlight, in full view of the castle, cape fluttering behind her, helmet visor locked down over her face. Blaze raised her sword.

"That's her!" cried the Rimefrost captain. "The portal! Come now, you cowards. Fight! Kill the princess!" A line of orcs charged from the city gates, weapons raised. The bait had worked.

Blaze sent a weaker flash toward one of the orcs that dissipated before it hit him. The orc sped up, as if escaping the fireball.

"She is weak! Send the gnolls," ordered the largest of the orc captains.

They have gnolls! A stab of fear hit Blaze. She tried to steel her nerves. *Focused, nonplussed, just like Princess Sapphire would be.*

War horns blared out across the city.

Moments later, a pack of wolf-like creatures half as high as the orcs burst out of the city gate.

"Oh my," said Blaze.

The gnolls were armed with shields and swords, their white fur bristling and their teeth gnashing, the snow churning in flurries as the pack charged toward Blaze, hopping logs and dodging trees as they ran through the forest. They bayed and howled as they ran, sending chills into Blaze's spine.

What they lacked in size, they made up for in sheer numbers and savagery. There was no chance her fire could stop *all* of the gnolls.

But she wasn't out of tricks yet.

She readied a small fireball in each hand, each one more brimstone than flame. She stalled for a moment, then blasted the heavy, snow-laden branches on two trees just in front of the charging pack. The branches shook, then sprang upward, dropping their heavy snow contents onto the attacking gnolls.

Two gnolls were buried in the small avalanche. The next half dozen were thrown off course, scattering between the dense trees and losing their forward momentum. One of the gnolls smacked head-on into a tree trunk. He fell down, whimpering.

The other gnolls regrouped, bounding over a log. There were still so many of them.

Blaze turned and ran.

The distance to the tunnel entrance suddenly seemed much further than she thought.

But it had to be that way. That was the plan. They had to lead all of the orcs out of the city before Blaze disappeared.

As she sprinted ahead, Blaze could tell she wasn't going to make it.

She looked back over her shoulder. The orcs and several companies of kobolds were still massing at the gates. The gnolls were gaining on her.

I have to give them more time.

Blaze stopped short of the tunnel entrance. She still had two dozen yards to go.

The gnolls formed a semicircle around her, their weapons drawn. They growled.

"Bring it. I'm not out yet," said Blaze. She tried to stand tall like Princess Sapphire would.

The Kings Summons

Blaze lifted a large rock and summoned her fire from within. The rock melted instantly. "Magma Storm!"

Using a second heat wave to propel the molten rock, the brimstone jetted ahead, splitting into pieces and swirling in arcs in front of her.

The gnolls howled in pain, their fur singed. The closest gnoll's wooden shield caught fire, and he tossed it away into the snow. Two more gnolls turned and ran shrieking into the forest.

Blaze swirled the storm of brimstone in larger arcs.

A spear split the air and she dodged, barely missing its stone head as it planted into the snow where she had just stood.

She directed one of the brimstone fragments at the gnoll who had thrown the spear, catching him full in the chest and knocking him backward.

The horde of orcs, much slower than the gnolls, were just reaching the edge of the trees.

She was vastly outnumbered.

Kobold archers loosed a wave of arrows that arched overhead in the starlight.

Blaze tracked as many as she could. At the last second, she let loose another blast.

"Fire Wave!" she cried.

The wash of fire obliterated the arrows, turning them to ash in mid-air. The fallout drove back the rest of the gnolls.

Cries of "Ember Mage" and "Get the princess" rang through the night as more warriors joined the fight.

An orc captain charged to the front of the group, his war hammer drawn. He, just like the other orcs, would be keen to destroy the princess and break the prophecy. They'd want their names immortalized.

Blaze dodged back. At least his charge would keep the kobolds from loosing another barrage of arrows. She was running low on fire. That last burst had drained her considerably.

She looked to the city gates. Warriors were still crowded in the entrance haphazardly donning helmets and boots.

The orc captain swung his hammer narrowly missing Blaze's back. "Come on!" she cried. She dodged and rolled. How was she supposed to fight an orc captain while she was low on fire?

"Keeping all the fun to yourself?" said a voice behind her.

"Princess!" cried Blaze.

With a rush of horror, Blaze realized the actual Princess Sapphire was beside her. She must have followed her up the tunnel.

"You can't be here," said Blaze.

"Oh, yes I can." Princess Sapphire smiled, her eyes flashing.

She tossed the blue cloak aside and charged the orc captain. A slash of her sword sent him crippled to the ground as the orc horde closed in on her.

Blaze dug deep, squeezing her body for enough strength to hold the channel open.

"Rapid fire!"

She let loose a full auto stream of twelve fireballs that ripped into the enemy line. Each fireball left her colder as she recoiled from the percussive blasts.

The decimated line broke, leaving Princess Sapphire enough time to cut through the tall pine tree trunk with the glowing blue edge of her sword. She retreated back as the hundred feet crashed down, blocking the road with its dense branches and forcing the enemy warriors to run around it.

"Into the tunnel. Quickly," said the princess.

Blaze's bones ached with afterchill. She forced herself to move but fell to one knee.

Princess Sapphire grabbed her and hurled her toward the opening.

"You first," Blaze said. "I have to seal it."

Princess Sapphire didn't argue. She leapt into the tunnel opening and clambered down its steep steps. Blaze pulled the hatch after her and collapsed into the tunnel.

"Come on fire," muttered Blaze to herself.

Blaze reached up and summoned a last jet of fire from her finger, arc-welding the edge of the hatch to the iron tunnel casing in three spots.

"Might hold them for a minute," Princess Sapphire

said. "Now run!"

The royal order did nothing to speed Blaze's aching muscles.

Shivering, Blaze reached out and looped her arm through the princess's.

"Saving your bacon again," Princess Sapphire said. "You've really got to learn to do that yourself." There was a hint of a smile on Princess Sapphire's hardened face.

"Okay," Blaze whimpered. She reached out for Princess Sapphire, then Blaze's vision went black and her knees buckled.

Blaze reached out for something to grab onto and felt her fingers close around a handle as she fell.

Then suddenly, everything flashed white. Her fingers tightened, and warmth surged through her body. She leapt to her feet. Her eyes flew open.

In her hand was Princess Sapphire's other sword, the long one Princess Sapphire had kept with her. One Blaze had never touched before. The blue gem embedded in its hilt glowed a fiery blue, then white, the light surging up Blaze's arm and into her body like blue-white flames.

Princess Sapphire's jaw dropped. "That's not supposed to happen," she said. "You . . . you've tapped into . . ."

But Princess Sapphire never finished the thought. "No time for that now. We've got to move. Go!" she said.

The white fire soaked into Blaze's skin. Power coursed through her for a moment, then faded into an even warmth.

Princess Sapphire shoved Blaze ahead down the tunnel, then turned, swinging her sword through the tunnel brace beams, notching several wooden supports with a flurry of strikes.

A creak of metal sounded through the tunnel.

"They're coming," Blaze called.

"Almost." Princess Sapphire swung her sword in a direct overhead cut and stepped back.

The tunnel collapsed in a blast of dust and debris. Blaze coughed, trying to catch her breath. The cave-in didn't stop.

Princess Sapphire collided with Blaze as they raced away from the falling rocks and billowing dust clouds.

At the junction, Blaze followed Princess Sapphire left, toward the Foruk's Falls entrance.

A hundred feet later, steep steps led up to a hatch. Princess Sapphire pushed it open, and cold, foul air flooded the passage. Blaze peeked her head out.

They were in the middle of a garbage heap behind a tavern. A rotting fish skull stared Blaze in the face.

"Yuck," said Princess Sapphire as she climbed out and stepped over a pile of rotting cabbages. "But I suppose it is a good hiding place for a secret tunnel."

Blaze climbed out. She eyed the princess's glowing blue sword. "What happened?" she said, reaching out.

Princess Sapphire whipped her cape around the sword,

hiding it from view. "Not now." She looked thoughtful. "Later. But not now."

Blaze leaned over, supporting herself on her knees. She snapped her fingers. No spark. Touching the sword had pushed back most of the afterchill and let her escape, but she hadn't held it long enough. She would have to recharge.

She looked to Princess Sapphire, still dressed in Blaze's clothes and blue cloak, as the princess scanned the village, ready to leap into battle once again. For a moment, it was like Blaze was looking at a possible version of herself. Is that what Blaze could look like? A leader who had given herself to a larger cause? So brave. An unstoppable force that could topple armies. Could Blaze give up her life as a rogue for something like that? Would anyone even want her to?

Across the alley, two dwarves were locked in combat with an orc patrol. They were outnumbered two-to-one. It looked like they would fall before the princess could reach them.

But Princess Sapphire moved faster than seemed possible. She drew her sword and leapt to their aid, swinging down on the nearest orc's iron helmet. It clanged like a bell, and the orc fell flat on his face.

"Ah, hullo," said one of the dwarves. He ducked an ax blade. His belt buckle was unmistakable. It was Bort. "That one was mine. I'd called dibs!"

"She didn't know that," said Tort. He smashed his shield into an orc's gut. "She hasn't seen our list."

Princess Sapphire leapt backward. "You wrote a list?"

"Aye!" both twins cried. Bort pulled a scrap of parchment from his pocket and waved it in the air.

Fighting back-to-back, the dwarves whirled heavy axes in a devastating pirouette. The three remaining orcs dropped to the ground as the massive battle axes cleaved through their ranks.

That's why they call them the Thunder Twins, thought Blaze.

But the battle was far from over. Waves of Rimefrost Orcs poured out from the side streets.

Suddenly, a gnome—Blaze hadn't even known there were any nearby—leapt from a rooftop and bounced off an orc's head, shoving the orc's helmet down over its eyes. Another gnome pulled a rope snare tight around the orc's leg. A third gnome dropped a banana peel in front of its foot, while a fourth waited on the ground as the huge orc slipped on the banana peel and fell forward.

The gnome shoved two huge carrots up the fallen orc's nose and broke them off, while the fifth gnome delivered a gong-strike to the side of the orc's helmet with a small golf club.

"Gnomes rule!" it cheered in a high-pitched voice as the others quick-bound the orc in a flurry of padlocks and chains they pulled from under their clothing. In seconds the gnomes were searching for their next victim, bounding back up to a rooftop where their pointed hats formed another scheming circle as they laid their next stage of plans.

"Remarkable," Princess Sapphire said. She folded her arms and grinned.

The gnomes turned and ran along the rooftop, their quiet footsteps pattering away toward their next victim: a kobold shaman crouched behind a cart.

Blaze was just quick enough to notice one of the gnomes drop a stick of mining explosive into a molasses barrel. Another gnome lit it while three more pushed the barrel down the sloped roof. The gnomes leapt in silent cheers, pumping their fists, others expectantly plugging their ears with massive grins on their tiny round faces.

BOOM.

The ice kobold shaman was encased in caramelized molasses, a hard-shell coating of crystalized sugar that ensured a sweet end to whatever spell it had been conjuring.

After another exultant cheer of "Gnomes rule!" the bunch was back in a huddle.

Nearby, the Thunder Twins had wrestled down a kobold between them and heaved it into the bucket of an empty catapult.

A gnome conveniently appeared just in time to release the catapult's catch, but not before pasting a freshly painted "kick me" sign on the kobold's tail. The kobold shrieked like an angry pig as it soared out over the castle wall.

Blaze shook her head in amazement. "How did that gnome even get over there so fast?"

Princess Sapphire turned up her hands. "And I thought I had seen it all when it came to fighting styles."

The waves of Rimefrost Orcs had been broken or pushed back, until only small pockets of resistance remained. The fight within the walls was well in hand.

"We're ready to wrap things up here," said Princess Sapphire, with one last swish of her sword.

"What about the enemies outside the gate?" Blaze asked.

The princess pointed to a line of dwarf soldiers on the city wall. In unison the dwarves nocked arrows, drew, and fired.

"The dwarf archers will have reduced our foe's number by a fair margin. Unfortunately for the enemy, they lost the defensible high ground."

"But it's not high ground to an ice giant," Blaze said.

Princess Sapphire, her expression grave, gave a nod. "We have the city, but we cannot defend it."

A thought occurred to Blaze. "If you leave," Blaze said. "Cernonos would follow you. A princess is a higher prize than a city."

"A fact I have been aware of my entire life." She inhaled a heavy breath. "Any of my siblings could risk our lives foolishly and all of us would suffer."

"What? Didn't you just—"

"Go outside the gates to save you? It was a calculated risk."

Outside the gates—"Dreck!"

Blaze left the princess and raced across a square, past a row of battered shops, and onto the siege wall. She ran behind rows of dwarf soldiers until she came to the main gate.

Unmistakable in the retreating ranks of Rimefrost Orcs was a medium-size orc with monk's robe, bound head to foot in ropes.

They had captured Dreck.

Chapter 16

Everlight Express

It wouldn't have been hard for the retreating Rimefrost Orcs to discover that Dreck was not one of them. As soon as they'd had a chance to look at his tattoos up close, they would have known he was a member of the Crook-Eye tribe. A hostage was a sure way to keep from getting shot in the back by an arrow.

Princess Sapphire ran to the edge of the wall and peered out. "Dreck?"

A knot formed in Blaze's throat. "Cap-captured." What

did she care anyway? He was still an orc. He had deceived her one too many times.

Princess Sapphire slammed her fists against the stone. "I can't bear this. If we stay in the city, they will all die in the battle."

"And if we leave?" Blaze asked.

"The people may have a chance to flee. Cernonos won't divide his forces to chase after women and children. He'll go for the kill—me—and then head straight for Dwarfholm Bastion."

That made sense to Blaze. The people would have to pack well for their journey. They would need time. Heading out into the Frostbyte Reach unprepared was suicide.

Orktag the Crook-Eye Orc shaman ascended the stone stair to the top of the wall. He was limping.

"We have to slow Cernonos's army down," Blaze said. "We have to buy the people time. Is there any chance, any weakness we can exploit?"

Orktag ground his teeth. "The demon Cernonos used his own essence to activate the Iron Collar. Some believe him to be immortal. He claims to be a demigod. Either way, he will be weak until he reaches a spawning point. He'll need to recharge."

Princess Sapphire pointed to a dwarf soldier. "You, get a map. I want to know where every spawning point is within five miles of the line between Foruk's Falls and the

The Kings Summons

Black Blood Peak."

The look in her eye turned from concern to a determination as cold as forged steel. "Cernonos controls the jotnar. If we can stop him, there is a chance to save Foruk's Falls. But we must catch him off guard. We have to attack before he reaches the city." She turned to Blaze. "I want my armor back."

"I'm done playing princess for the day," Blaze said. She and the princess exchanged clothing in a guardhouse and emerged just as a dwarf wearing pewter-rimmed spectacles unrolled a leather map onto the stonework of the city wall.

As Blaze leaned over to look at the Foruk's Fall's tactical map, a freyjan handed her the blue robe the princess had left near the tunnel entrance, muttering some apology about its condition.

Blaze lifted the robe to sweep it over her shoulders, then paused. The robe was a wreck. It was torn in several places and stained with grime and soot from her journey and the battles she'd fought since she'd arrived at the Frostbyte Reach. The robe had provided extra warmth. The Reach at night was brutally cold, and she still ached from the afterchill.

Once, the robe of the Ember Mage had made her superior. Like that staff, the blue ember robe had set her above the ordinary people.

Around her, dwarf soldiers wearing plain brown fur-lined coats stood shoulder to shoulder along the battlements. All the same, and none of them seemed to care that they were no different from the others—glad to stand and fight together.

I would be one of them, she thought, knowing that she couldn't. She wasn't a dwarf or even from the Reach.

Why had she always insisted on fighting alone? Here was an army worth fighting with, a cause worth fighting for.

Without a word, she slipped away from Princess Sapphire and the spontaneous war council and stepped toward the watch fire.

Gripping the cloth of her ember cloak, she plunged her hands into the flames. The cloth turned yellow, then white, and finally flaked away in bits of red-rimmed ash that rose in the heated plume and drifted over the city toward the frozen river below the famed ice-bound falls.

"What are you doing?"

Blaze turned to see the princess standing up and staring at her. A gap had appeared between the dwarf captains. She stepped over the map and moved close enough to share a private conversation. "Blaze?"

"I'm . . . cleaning up," she said.

The princess glanced down at the fire. "Do you think ember robes grow on trees? That's a mark of your Order."

How could she explain this to the princess? Princess Sapphire had been the one who had saved her, the one who had promised that she would be an Ember Mage.

The Kings Summons

I was.

"Princess Sapphire, do you . . . do you remember me?" Blaze asked. She had to know. She had to have the courage to ask. "I'm Blaze . . . from Midway?"

The flames of the watch fire seemed to freeze. Even the war council and the entire wall guard seemed to hold still, eavesdropping until they heard an answer.

"Midway," Princess Sapphire nodded. She did not hesitate. "The girl with the spark."

Had she known this whole time?

"Yes," Blaze said. "And you told me someday I'd become an Ember Mage. You promised it."

Princess Sapphire spoke, "And I see you have."

Blaze shook her head. "No. I'm . . . I am not a member of the Order of Ember," Blaze said. She didn't care who heard it. It was time she spoke the truth. "That's why I don't have a staff."

The princess seemed surprised.

"Haven't you seen my eyes when I summon fire?" Blaze said. "Red—like the demons from the spawning points. Like the jotnar after it was captured. Red!"

Princess Sapphire studied Blaze's face. Her blue eyes were piercing, like they were looking so deep into Blaze, they were seeing her past.

"So you were banished. What did you do?" asked Princess Sapphire.

"A sparring match—one of the usual upstarts trying

to challenge me," Blaze shook her head. "The instructors knew better than to test my strength. But the new mages and the apprentices—they all wanted a shot at the prodigy, the girl with the red eyes." Blaze tasted the bitter words on her tongue. "And what could I do about it? He knew what I was capable of."

"Who?" asked the princess.

"One of the older boys. He was trying to prove himself." Blaze wrapped her arms around herself, feeling a lot smaller than she had a moment before.

The princess folded her own arms, standing like a mother, or a judge waiting to hear the tale and pass down a sentence.

A lump formed in Blaze's throat. "I was supposed to channel my attack to his staff—it's far easier to absorb fire that way."

"You didn't."

Princess Sapphire's abrupt manner made the whole confession a lot easier.

Blaze nodded.

"And?"

"He was . . . he didn't defend well."

"Dead?"

Blaze shook her head. "No. But he won't ever be the same—blind." Tears found their way into Blaze's eyes.

"And so it was your fault," the princess concluded. "Wholly and completely."

The Kings Summons

Blaze bit her trembling lip. Now the tears ran in two streams down her cheeks. "Yes." The word escaped like a dagger being drawn out of her. "I was too angry. I was too out of control. I hurt people when I don't mean to." Blaze had confessed her failure to the very person who had promised her success, the first person to believe in her.

The princess in blue-tinged armor folded her arms and stared coldly. Now she knew. The "Ember Mage" her father had sent was no eminent magician, but an outcast. One of the wall guards glanced over. Now they all knew.

"And the Crook-Eyes?" asked the princess.

Blaze started. She wasn't sure what Princess Sapphire meant by that. It must have shown in her face.

"The Crook-Eye tribe. You've made your peace with them," said Princess Sapphire. It was more of a command than a question. Blaze winced. It certainly felt like the princess was seeing right through her. Blaze didn't know how to answer that.

"I . . ." said Blaze. She wasn't sure she could finish her sentence: . . . *am just getting to that.*

But was she? Was she really? Blaze couldn't honestly say she was.

And then, Princess Sapphire simply nodded. "Are you with us or with them?" she asked.

Blaze thought before she answered. She wasn't fighting for Cernonos or the Rimefrost Orcs. She certainly wasn't on the side of the Dark Consul. But was she really *with*

Princess Sapphire? Could she really swear her allegiance to an alliance that included the Crook-Eye tribe? She had always fought alone. This would change everything.

She would have to commit. She would have to forgive. Right now, she couldn't do that.

Blaze took a shaky breath. A spark lit within her and then faded, something different, something new and utterly strange.

It faded, and in the moment, she thought of Dreck. Such a silly, simple orc-monk. He made it so hard to hate him. And now he was captured by the enemy, and this time they knew he wasn't one of them.

"I'm not sure," said Blaze. She couldn't meet Princess Sapphire's eyes.

"You can't fight alone forever, Blaze," said Princess Sapphire. Blaze wanted to reply, but she still couldn't find the words.

Bort and Tort barreled past her and dove nearly headfirst into the war council. "What's this—gambling without us?" said Bort.

"Oh—not planning!" Tort moaned.

"You two—stay," Princess Sapphire ordered. "This is our only chance to save Foruk's Falls. We must stop Cernonos. He controls the jotnar."

Blaze pushed her hands in her pockets and stepped between the stout and warm-looking dwarves. It was strange standing next to dwarf adolescents with bushy, black beards. Their helmets came level with her chin.

"A covert strike is our best chance," Princess Sapphire said. "He needs to recharge at a spawning point. He'll be vulnerable then."

"But after—" Blaze called over to the huddled group.

The princess spoke over her. "We wait until he gets to the spawning point and starts the recharging process, if he hasn't already," she said. "He'll be open to an attack then, especially one from behind."

"That is nuts," said Tort. "With respect, Your Majesty."

Bort reached around behind Blaze and slapped the back of his brother's helmet. "How is that respectful?" He gave a belch to emphasize the point.

"Blaze, I know you want to go after the hostages," Princess Sapphire said, shaking her head. "But we can't divide our forces. We have one goal—Cernonos. He goes down, so does his control of the jotnar."

The words came with another stab of pain.

"Great," said Blaze.

Princess Sapphire, crouching with one knee on the ground, gave a sigh. "This isn't the best plan—it isn't really a plan at all . . . more a prayer." She gestured to the city. "A jotnar can knock down these walls like building blocks—freeze entire city blocks. I shudder to think what a dark jotnar, fueled by rage and hate, can do. I know how hard we worked to free the city. But for anyone who stays, these walls will be their tomb. We have to take the fight to Cernonos."

Bort grunted. "Sounds good." Tort swung his ax up to his shoulder. "When do we start?"

Princess Sapphire pointed at them. "I like that attitude. Gather your men. We leave in ten minutes at the west gate. Let the soldiers make their goodbyes. Leave none to guard the city."

She turned to the dwarf with the spectacles. "You're the Jarl here, I assume?"

"Yes, my lady," he said.

"Order the evacuation of the entire district. No one takes the Torch Road. They'll be expecting that. It's too dangerous and there's no chance of escape if Cernonos's army catches you inside those tunnels. Flee to the plains or Dwarfholm Bastion with as little as possible. The dark jotnar will spare no women or children. The collar it wears is a thing of evil made for destruction."

"Yes, Princess. I shall see to it." The Jarl summoned his captain of the guard, who summoned a sergeant, who gave three long blasts on his horn. Heads popped out through windows and doors as the recently freed villagers exchanged looks of disbelief.

"The dark jotnar approaches," cried the sergeant. "By order of the Jarl, the city must be evacuated immediately. None shall stay. Flee to Midway or Dwarfholm. Wear as much warm clothing as you can. Take supplies to make fire. Pack food for the journey. But take no cart or wagon—only what you can carry on your backs."

"Princess," Blaze asked. She was just so tired. She didn't think she could walk another step. "How are we going to make that journey now? We've been up all night and the day before. We can't stop to rest—but I'm so tired I can barely . . . what are you smiling about?"

"You've never ridden the Everlight Express?" said the princess. She was grinning from ear to ear. She beckoned for Blaze to follow her.

Blaze followed Princess Sapphire, surrounded by several dozen dwarf soldiers and Crook-Eye Orcs to the west gate. But they did not go through it. Princess Sapphire turned aside toward what looked like a battered, old, emerald-green barn just inside the closed city gate.

"We disguised the entrance when the orcs came," explained a dwarf with a poufy hat. He opened the barn door. They had swept the straw into a mound on one side and opened a trapdoor in the floor. Beneath it were stone steps that spiraled downward and softly burning oil lamps on the walls. A low whistle sounded from deep in the earth.

The soldiers clambered down the steps in a rush of clanking armor, disappearing from view.

"What is this place?" asked Blaze.

Princess Sapphire motioned down the steps. "See for yourself."

Blaze *was* curious. So she descended the spiral stair

after the soldiers. It went down several flights until she could hear the soldier's voices and the hiss of machinery. She took the last flight of steps three at a time and rounded the corner.

The staircase opened up into a large, hollow cavern with a low ceiling.

A long platform made of carefully laid stonework stretched into the darkness on either side. A few feet in front of that was a tunnel. And at the edge of the platform, sitting on a pair of rails, was a line of wooden carriages linked together and painted emerald green with golden trim. Someone flipped a switch, and the whole train lit up with bright, warm golden light. The steel wheels glowed. Even the rails lit up like slender tails of shooting stars, streaking off into the darkness of the tunnel.

A whistle blew, and the steam engine began to turn.

"All aboard!" shouted someone from the main engine.

A conductor hurried over to Blaze and Princess Sapphire. "Welcome to the Everlight Express," he said, his smile beaming. He held out a hand. "Tickets, please."

Princess Sapphire folded her arms and glared. She looked about as accommodating as a rattlesnake.

"Right then—no tickets," he said, looking down at the floor. "To your coaches. Next stop Black Blood Peak foothills on the . . . the . . . unfinished line."

"We wouldn't normally travel that far down the line, but these are dire circumstances," said the princess.

206

The Kings Summons

"That doesn't sound good," Blaze muttered under her breath.

"Perfectly safe," Tort said, bustling past her. "So long as it stops before the gap."

"What gap?" asked Blaze.

"The one where the track ends right before a bottomless pit ten fathoms deep," said Bort.

Tort whacked him on the back of the head. "How can it be *bottomless* if it's ten fathoms deep, numb-beard?" he asked.

"Perfectly safe!" Bort echoed, clapping Blaze on the back. "Now choose our coach. We've got six hours for rest and relaxation—do I smell braised mutton?"

"Yes!" she said. The smell of the warm meal set her stomach churning in expectation.

Blaze hurried along the train and hopped into a coach near the rear with Princess Sapphire. The small fighting force filled most of the train of coaches, but there were enough empty seats to give Blaze and the princess their own coach.

Princess Sapphire climbed the steps and opened a hatch. Inside were four dwarf-sized plush seats facing each other and two bunks overhead. Apparently, the dwarves of the Frostbyte Reach didn't mind sleeping in close quarters. The cabin was inviting and by far the most comfortable, cozy-looking place Blaze had seen since leaving the king's castle in Crystalia.

Blaze paused at the threshold. "What about them?" asked Blaze, nodding to the city above. "Shouldn't we take the villagers with us?"

Princess Sapphire shook her head. "We've filled most of the seats. I know this looks like comfort, Blaze, and it is, but these tunnels do not lead to safe havens. They lead to the enemy. We are going into battle. They're better off out there in the Reach. They'll find their way."

"I suppose . . ." said Blaze. She felt guilty.

"Blaze, you're a soldier. And I need you to be at your best when we launch our next attack. And that means getting proper sleep."

"Maybe I could get used to this," said Blaze. She really did need some rest. She followed Princess Sapphire inside and settled into one of the plush velvet seats. She practically melted into it, it was so soft.

"There's nothing quite like it," said Princess Sapphire. "And right now, this is what our soldiers need most." That made more sense to Blaze.

Princess Sapphire lit a small coal stove in the car as the train began moving forward with a clickety-clack sound.

The train paused for a split second, then lurched ahead on the tracks, pressing Blaze backward into her seat.

"What's pulling us?" Blaze asked.

"A gear system fed by underground streams. Quite ingenious—if a little loud," said Princess Sapphire.

"Yeah, but it's wonderful," Blaze said. She had never

experienced anything like it. It wasn't the uncontrolled roll of mine cars. Nor was it the methodical plodding of a pack mule. It was something new entirely. To be carried up a mountain tunnel by a metal carriage—it was like magic.

The conductor's voice sounded through a pipe. "Expected arrival in five hours, fifty minutes."

"Our route is meandering since the carriage train can't climb the steep canyon," the princess explained. "Should be long enough for a short nap."

She opened a drawer and withdrew a silky blue nightgown. The warrior princess wasted no time in throwing off her armor, changing into the nightgown, and tucking herself into one of the upper bunks. It was the most incongruous sight Blaze had ever seen—a warrior climbing into a soft bunk in a nightgown. She had always suspected that Princess Sapphire slept in her armor.

Blaze opened her drawer and found the dwarf-sewn silk to be the finest thing she had ever worn. "Are all the coaches this fancy?"

"Of course," the princess said, her eyes closed. "When dwarves travel to visit one another, it's a big deal. They might stay for months, sharing memories and writing memoirs, debating and playing games, and building new homes. A trip is a thing to remember."

The night gown was billowy but short enough to tickle Blaze's knees. With the stove keeping the room toasty warm, Blaze climbed onto her bunk and let her head hit the pillow.

But as tired as she was, she wasn't able to sleep just yet. Her mind was still racing from all that had happened: escaping down the Torch Road, Foruk's Falls, the Iron Collar. Now that she had a moment of quiet, her thoughts were catching up to her.

She stared out the window of the train at the passing surface of the tunnel. The occasional stalactite zipped by, followed by openings in the cavern. Bright flashes of blue, green, and white appeared in the window, then were gone.

Blaze sat up in her bunk. "Princess, what was that?" she asked.

Princess Sapphire suppressed a yawn. She turned over in her bunk opposite Blaze and rubbed her eyes. She barely glanced out the window as another flash of green passed by.

This time Blaze saw more: the flashes of color came from pools of steaming, glowing liquid.

"Ah, we're deep beneath the surface here," said Princess Sapphire. "Closer to the core of Crystalia." The cavern opened up wider than it ever had, and several shimmering blue and green pools came into view. There was even a white one as big as a pond, its surface shimmering like glass, and deep below, what looked like a glowing diamond.

"It's magnificent," whispered Blaze.

"Some of the loremasters think that when we're deeper

underground, we're closer to the heart of Crystalia, and therefore, closer to the Goddess's essence," Princess Sapphire said. "The Goddess is fueled by compassion and binding things together, not tearing them apart." She rolled over to face Blaze and pulled back the edge of her quilt. Underneath was her sword. The gem on its hilt pulsed blue. It was brighter than Blaze had ever seen it.

"My sword draws its magic from the core of Crystalia. I think that when you touched it back in the tunnels, you tapped into that core for a brief moment. That's what allowed you to overcome the afterchill. It's the best theory I've got, anyway."

The glowing pools disappeared from view and the tunnel went dark again as the Everlight Express sped onward. Blaze laid her head on her pillow and stared up at the ceiling.

"There's one thing I don't get," she said. "Back in Midway, those Crook-Eye Orcs attacked me and my village. They tried to *kill* you. And now you're working with them? What happened?"

"I spared their lives," said Princess Sapphire. "I let them go, and they saw that Crystalia doesn't have to be full of vengeance. That made them into allies. And wouldn't you know it? One of those warriors had a son. I had spared his father's life."

Blaze felt the fire within begin to crackle. It wanted to roar. "I wish my parents were so lucky," she said.

"So do I," Princess Sapphire sniffed. She sounded like she was about to cry. Blaze didn't think that was possible. Not from battle-hardened Princess Sapphire.

"But—" said Blaze. She wanted to shout. She wanted to scream.

"That warrior's son was Dreck, Blaze," said Princess Sapphire. She was stern again. "I lost my own mother when I was very young. But you being an orphan does not justify making *more* of them."

Blaze said nothing. The fire within simmered and boiled. How could she forget about that day? It had shaped her. The pain had made her who she was.

The train rattled on, keeping rhythm with her thoughts.

Then Princess Sapphire spoke, "There are other sources of magic besides anger, Blaze."

Then it was quiet.

In her dreams Blaze saw the dark jotnar's red eyes confront her, blazing with hate, burning with destructive power unknown since the cursing of Arcadia.

She dreamt of Dreck's oafish elegance. She dreamt of Midway and the halls of the Order of Ember, of Crystalia Castle, and of the creeping Nether Realms bleeding into Crystalia from the Midnight Tower, the mist of darkness seeping from the spawning points, and the goat-hoofed demon Cernonos.

Then she dreamt of nothing.

The Kings Summons

Blaze was jolted awake by the conductor's voice. "Breakfast is served."

A hatch in the carriage's roof opened, and for a moment, the train's clacking sounded loudly. The dimly glowing lamp in the ceiling brightened, and a metal-cased box lowered on a string. When the box hit the floor, a catch released, the hook retracted, and the roof snapped shut.

"The twins' brother Gork invented the food delivery system," the princess said as she sat up on her bunk. The food smelled incredible.

Princess Sapphire retrieved the box and climbed up to Blaze's bunk. They ate breakfast in bed: roast mutton, sweet crumpets, and hot tea.

"When the rest of Crystalia hears about how the dwarves run carriages underground, the whole Reach will be overrun with travelers," said Blaze.

"They have to get to the Reach first," Princess Sapphire said. "And the dwarves won't build a line to connect Arcadia or the Fae Wood—too much pride, and too much work. And to tell the truth, they have to pay the gnomes from Clockwork Cove to engineer most of it—they hate that."

"Arrival in ten minutes," announced the conductor through the intercom pipe. "Please prepare for disembarking—

let us pray the autowinders stop before the gap."

Blaze sat bolt up. "That's not very reassuring coming from the conductor," she said.

Princess Sapphire was already dressed and buckling her sword belt. "Better get dressed then. Going to battle in that nightgown?" she asked.

Blaze flapped the lacey sleeves. "I'd probably burn this up. Better change." She slipped out of the nightgown and threw on her trousers and tunic. The princess tossed her a coat from the tall, narrow closet at the back of the coach.

"This? Is it for the opera?" Blaze looked in a hand mirror set in the wall. The bulky coat was made of snow ferret fur. "Snow ferrets—those are fireproof." The nimble rascals were nearly impossible to eradicate. Their more aggressive cousins in the Dragonback Peaks were known to eat lava and spit it at trespassers.

"Appropriate for a coach with its own fireplace," the princess noted.

That made sense.

"On the map, the unfinished Everlight Express station appears to be slightly uphill from the nearest spawning point on the way from Cernonos's camp to Foruk's Falls," Princess Sapphire explained.

"No wonder the station isn't finished," Blaze said.

"Yes, the enemy's advance has changed many plans. It's time we changed theirs."

"How?" Blaze asked.

The Kings Summons

"The canyon has only a few access points, and this spawning point is by far easiest to reach," said Princess Sapphire. "Once Cernonos gives the orders to march on Foruk's Falls, all eyes will be forward. Then we bring everything we've got to bear on Cernonos—every arrow, flame, and sword. We fight like our lives depend on it."

The danger was real, not only to the warriors but to the entire realm. Under no circumstances could the princess's life be put in jeopardy. *Is this—too much of a risk?* Of course it was. But unless they pulled together, there was no hope of saving any thread in the tapestry of the Goddess.

"When we arrive, we'll need your fire to take down any minions. Don't get distracted by Cernonos," said Princess Sapphire.

"Yes, Your Majesty."

"And don't die either."

Blaze nodded.

"And don't get captured."

Blaze shrugged. "Should I take notes?"

The coach slowed, then began to shudder violently. Blaze steadied herself against the bed.

"Hold on to something!" shouted Princess Sapphire. Something was seriously wrong.

The conductor's voice shouted through the intercom, "Attention all passengers, we have full autowinder failure; the gears aren't going to stop us fast enough. Please prepare to disembark at the platform."

The carriage shuddered again, and the conductor shouted two final words: "Abandon train!"

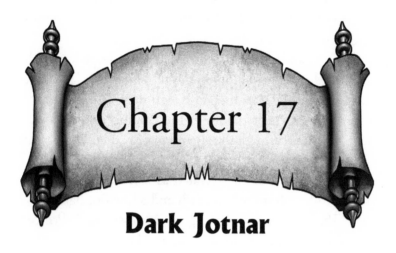

Chapter 17

Dark Jotnar

Princess Sapphire hurled the door to their coach open. There was a wide, open cavern with a flat platform speeding by just a few feet from the train. Princess Sapphire hurled herself from the open door, tucking and rolling as she skidded across the flagstones. Blaze didn't know if she could follow suit, when she saw the end of the platform. The cave wall was approaching fast. She was running out of platform.

Ignoring the fear inside her, Blaze grit her teeth and

dove from the train. She slid across the flat stones, rolling and skidding as she landed, the soft fur coat cushioning the impact just a little.

All around, round-bellied dwarves leapt from the train and rolled to a stop on the platform. The larger orcs merely took the leap and landed on their feet at a run.

At the front of the train, the conductor took a wild leap. He flew through the air and plastered himself against a "Danger" sign.

The empty train accelerated as it moved out of view, followed by a horrendous crash and a burst of flame.

"There goes the Everlight Express," said Princess Sapphire. "Is the conductor going to be—"

"He'll be all right," Tort said gruffly. "He can hike back down the tunnel." He raised his ax and then stared at Blaze. "Where are you going—the opera?"

Bort gave her an approving once-over. "I love a mage with style. I hope you brought your flame to this dance."

Blaze balled up her fists. "Let's smoke this monster," she said.

The princess moved to the front of the group. "Silence in the ranks." She drew her sword and readied her shield. The dwarves and orcs immediately fell into rank. "Our best estimate puts the spawning point only a few hundred yards downhill from the concealed entrance to the station. We can only guess what we will face outside. Follow my lead. Attack when I attack. Don't stop, even if I fall.

Cernonos's control of the dark jotnar must be broken. It is the only hope for saving the Reach."

Princess Sapphire raced silently up the steps, followed by the swiftest of the Crook-Eye Orcs. Blaze hurried to keep pace. *Unfortunately for you, Princess,* she thought as she came even with Princess Sapphire, *I came here for a reason.* If it came down to victory or to saving her life, Blaze would save the princess.

The rush of impending battle made Blaze's palms tingle with sweat as heat rose up her spine and neck. Nearing the top of the stairs, she lit the spark, and a rush of heat coursed through her. The air around Blaze's hands warped as the world took on an angry red hue. There was time for feeling sorry for one's mistakes, a time for looking back, and even a time for rest.

There was also a time for rage.

"It's payback time," said Blaze.

They rounded the corner and were met with a wall of packed snow. The exit to the station was buried.

At a glance from the princess, Blaze stepped forward. She calmed herself, focusing her pent-up thermal energy, then released a jet of fire from her hand.

It was too wide. She needed more focus. She needed it to cut, not melt.

Controlling strong fire so tightly was a skill few Ember Mages mastered at a young age.

Blaze closed her eyes. *Come on.* She opened her eyes

again.

The fire swelled and then narrowed into a tight plasma column as she straightened her hands.

She moved the jet of flame across the face of the drift, cutting a body-width slot in the hard-packed snow.

Blaze fed her stream of fire until the snow was thin enough that light shown through from the outside.

She kicked at the snow. It broke away in a clump, revealing the mid-morning sun's sparkling brightness. Light flooded the tunnel. She stepped out into the open daylight.

What Blaze saw was worse than she'd imagined. They had made a crucial miscalculation: the spawning point wasn't a few hundred yards away.

It was only two dozen.

In the center of a clearing of ice and rock, black mist streamed out from a collection of stone pillars that had collapsed into the shape of a serpent's gaping jaw. All around the scene, ice curled in tortured shapes, mingled with rust, tar, and ash. Black tar vomited up from the earth.

Fear congealed in Blaze's veins, freezing her limbs.

A band of Rimefrost Orcs and a dozen gnolls surrounded the perimeter. In the center, just a few feet away, the black mist poured into the open mouth and nostrils of a huge creature with cloven feet and black horns protruding from his head.

Cernonos.

The Kings Summons

Already the runes on his armor glowed red with the Dark Realm's magic. He had already recharged. They were too late.

Blaze felt paralyzed. She was helpless in the face of such a monster.

She had to turn back into the tunnel. She had to run. But several Crook-Eye Orcs and the ranks of dwarves were piled up behind her. There was no going back.

"Now, Blaze," the princess's voice sounded in her ear like a whip cracking.

Fear, if unchecked, could kill her inner flame. Blaze needed raw anger.

Blaze reached deep. The surge rose within her.

"Now," said Princess Sapphire.

Blaze turned, stretched out her hands and blasted the tunnel opening wide enough for three orcs to emerge at the same time.

Blaze could feel the fire within rising. Her reserves were building up. She charged forward. Dwarves and orcs streamed out of the tunnel behind her.

"Attack!" cried Princess Sapphire.

Cernonos turned, his horns twisting in her direction.

It was takedown time.

"Recoil Fireball!"

In three seconds, Blaze unleashed several concussive fireballs at the pillar behind Cernonos. The shots erupted on impact like gnomish mining sticks.

The demon sneered as the fireballs whizzed past.

They slammed into a fragment of stone at the pillar's base. It cracked under the weight of the ten-ton pillar and sent the twenty-foot-high stone column toppling down toward Cernonos.

Cernonos turned and raised his arms to shove the falling stone aside. If it landed on him, he would be trapped.

Blaze spun around as more dwarves charged from the tunnel.

Where was that dark jotnar?

And for that matter, where was Dreck?

Blaze charged forward toward the center of the spawning point, trying to keep a pillar between her and Cernonos as more Crook-Eye Orcs piled out from the station's secret entrance.

Cernonos bent under the pillar's weight. Then he pressed up off his shoulder and tossed it aside.

Great Goddess!

Cernonos's human-like eyes widened in excitement as he tracked Princess Sapphire's unmistakable silver-blue armor. He opened his mouth and unleashed a torrent of fire. But instead of orange, it was black flame.

Princess Sapphire crouched behind her shield—it could only last seconds in that blast's furnace heat.

Blaze couldn't let her die. She had to do something.

Blaze dove in front of the princess and tapped the

stream, letting the demon's magic mingle with her own in a dangerous co-channeling. Stretching her arms to the sides, Blaze parted the fire stream, which curled up and dissipated, leaving enough room for the orcs and dwarves to fan out on either side of the demon.

He was about to be surrounded.

With a cry of rage, Cernonos roared for his minions. "Kill them!"

Before the Rimefrost Orcs and gnolls could respond, a hail of whistling arrows from all sides descended upon the monster. The arrowheads pulsed with magic. Blue lightning from each of the arrows shot outward, combining into a net of electricity that collapsed around Cernonos.

Cernonos bowed under the crushing attack, his muscles convulsing from the electric shock.

"It's working," cried Princess Sapphire.

Then the demon thrust his arms outward, obliterating the lightning net. Residual sparks ran over his body and into the ground. He reached outward, his fingers elongating into black tendrils. He thrashed his tendril arms, lashing out across the clearing. The black tendrils caught the dwarf archers, wrapping around their throats, lifting them into the air, and slamming them against the pillars.

Crook-Eye Orcs raced past the archers, flanking Cernonos and cutting off his retreat.

Cernonos's attention was on the forces at the perimeter.

This was their chance.

Princess Sapphire saw it too. She ran forward. Blaze raced by her side—she could divert his fire. But before Blaze could raise her hands to muster a defense, the demon lunged forward, sweeping his long, black horns down at the princess.

Blaze was caught in the vee between two horns and thrown aside. She landed in a snow bank and climbed to her feet, her body steaming and sizzling. Nearby, the princess lay face down ten feet away at the base of a pillar, helmet askew, hands limp. A dash of blood on the pillar matched a red spot on the princess's hair.

"Princess Sapphire!" called Blaze.

The princess didn't stir.

Cernonos didn't even know we were coming, and he still has the upper hand.

Following the princess's orders, the orcs and dwarves continued their assault. They had come up inside the Rimefrost Orcs' defensive perimeter. By the time the enemy came to Cernonos's aid, it could be too late.

Orc swords and Bort and Tort's whirling axes hacked through the tendrils, releasing the captive archers. The perimeter around Cernonos was closing fast.

A shadow moved across the scene, turning all from sparkling light to ominous black.

The dark jotnar.

They had to get out of there—and fast. Most

importantly, Blaze had to get Princess Sapphire to safety.

Blaze grabbed Princess Sapphire's sword, quickly slid it into her belt, then lifted Princess Sapphire under her shoulders and dragged her back toward the station entrance.

With all that heavy armor, she was barely moveable.

Blaze had to get her out of there. The Prophecy depended on it.

She looked up as the jotnar's enormous form towered over the tree line. It was so tall; the treetops barely reached its chest. Runes on its skin glowed red.

It was too late.

The dark jotnar raised a hand, and a burst of ice and snow shot toward the Crook-Eye Orcs who had flanked Cernonos. When the ice flurries settled, the loyal orcs were encased in several feet of solid ice. They hadn't even had time to react before they were frozen still.

The jotnar's other hand let fly another ice blast toward the dwarves, sweeping from one side to the other. Princess Sapphire's tiny army was buried in a wall of ice.

Cernonos laughed.

He had won. As bold as Blaze and Princess Sapphire and their band of orcs and dwarves had been, they were still no match for the jotnar. It had been all too easy for him.

But Blaze could do nothing to help. She dragged Princess Sapphire back toward the station. Cernonos's head turned, following the tell-tale tracks in the snow left by Princess Sapphire's body.

Blaze had to get them out of there, and fast. She knelt in the snow, one hand still gripping Princess Sapphire's armor, the other placed flat on a dark blue spot in the snow near the base of the cliff. The snow would be weak there—or so Blaze hoped. She forced heat out of her palm in a burst, then held it. The snow melted, then shifted, and finally broke. She fell two feet, pulling the princess with her.

She turned to see Cernonos looking at his feet, where there were several sticks of gnomish explosive.

Bort and Tort—they had lit the fuses before getting hit by the ice.

BOOM. BOOM.

Two explosions rocked the amphitheater.

Cernonos reeled backward as the ice walls encasing the dwarves rippled with spider-vein cracks.

Blaze looked up to see a wall of snow collapsing toward her. Frantically she hauled Princess Sapphire back. But it was too late.

"Fire Wave!" cried Blaze. She let fly a burst of heat that turned the falling snow into a gust of steam. Hidden by the steam and collapsing snow, she unleashed another wave of heat into the snow below her. The snow collapsed, and both of them fell several feet, tumbling and bouncing into the darkness.

226

The Kings Summons

Then it was all darkness and cold. Blaze had managed to hold onto the pauldron on the princess's armor. She felt around in the snow. The princess was still there, but they were trapped in a small hollow underneath the snow.

Don't panic. Keep a cool head. The princess was still breathing—barely.

They were deep enough, and it was dark enough, Blaze was pretty sure they had fallen into some sort of tunnel.

She took a deep breath. Her best hope was that it was connected to the main tunnel they'd just come from.

She lit a small fireball in her hand—just enough to cast an orange glow through the ice. They were in a hollow just barely wide enough for Blaze to stretch her arms out. She pressed her hand against the ice at her feet and pushed her inner heat outward. The ice melted into a pool. She pressed harder until it vaporized into steam, and the ice began to creak.

There was no time for this. Blaze wound up her arms and threw two successive fireballs into the ice, then three more in rapid succession. The ice broke, and they both fell again with a lurch.

This time, they landed in a pack of snow. Blaze let loose again, this time with a stream of flame, carving out a path beneath her. It was exhausting work. And all the more frustrating since she didn't know exactly where they were going—she was just making the best guess she could. She didn't know how much fire she had left.

The snow broke, and they fell once more onto something hard and flat. Blaze pulled herself close to Princess Sapphire's limp body, then lit a fireball so she could look around.

She was sitting on a wooden plane that looked something like a roof. *The Everlight Express*. They had found their way back to the train—or what was left of it.

The belt-driven gears whirred steadily on either side of the tracks. They must not be that far from the platform. Blaze shot a weak fireball ahead into the darkness.

She was wrong. Beyond the edge of the carriage was a gaping, black pit—they were all the way to the gap. The tracks ended abruptly at the edge of a deep crevice in the rock, an underground seam twenty yards across. The half-finished footings for a bridge protruded from the cliff face below her.

Blaze fed heat into the fireball in her hand so she could see even further into the darkness. Luckily, the front of the train had struck the opposite side of the gap and backed up, suspending the carriages dangerously between the two cliff faces. She stood on one of the last few cars still resting on the track. If the car hadn't been tangled in a wreckage of twisted metal, they too would likely have plunged into the gap.

Blaze opened the second-to-last car and struggled to haul Princess Sapphire over the edge of the roof into the carriage. She shut the door and waited in silence, her

228

panting breath the only sound in the darkness.

She huddled, her knees pulled up to her chin, shivering in the cold. How close was Cernonos? She didn't think he would have been able to follow her down here. Their escape had been covered up in the chaos. At least she hoped so.

But what about the Crook-Eye Orcs and the dwarf soldiers? Their little army was frozen solid in ice. How long could they survive? Dwarves were said to be like fish—they could thaw after a freeze. But what about the orcs?

She looked to Princess Sapphire's empty scabbard. She must have lost her other sword in the battle above. Blaze had tapped into it once, for a moment. If only she had that now.

Silent tears fell down her cheeks, then froze to her skin. They had failed. And they'd almost lost Princess Sapphire in the process. Cernonos and the dark jotnar were just too powerful. And now Foruk's Falls would fall.

The insides of the carriage walls were frozen over with a thin layer of frost. What had once been a cozy carriage now felt like a tomb. If she didn't find warmth, she would freeze to death. If she lit a fire, she might give away their hiding place.

One peril for another.

Finally, when she could barely feel her fingers, and the shivering had become uncontrollable, Blaze lit the small coal stove with her spark.

She nursed the coals until they were a tiny nugget of orange heat. She pressed her hands close, drawing heat from the coals, then shaping it carefully into flames. A few degrees of warmth and a tiny, precious glow seeped into the coach. Blaze shut the iron grate on the stove.

She dragged the princess closer to the heat. Motion caught Blaze's eye. The plate armor on Princess Sapphire's chest rose and fell. Then it rose and fell again, in a slow, regular movement.

Thank the Goddess—she was alive.

Suddenly, the stove flared and the grate blasted open. Heat rushed into Blaze as bright orange flames leapt outward into the carriage, filling the room.

Startled, Blaze scrambled backward. The flames danced and flickered until their center drew back into a single column and formed the outline of a woman in a cloak. It held out its hands, then crackled as it spoke.

"Blaze of Midway," it said, heat and light rushing from the woman's form, "It is time to return to the Order of Ember."

Chapter 18

Fire Vision

It was the Archmage herself. Her voice crackled like wood in a campfire. There was a familiar flicker of color behind her—the red rock of the Dragonback Peaks.

"I'm here, Archmage," Blaze said. Her heart pounded within her. *What could this mean? Had they called to give her help? To chastise her?*

"We have watched from afar," said the Archmage. Her face came into view, a mix of shadow and flame. "And we are pleased," she said. The figures of the council formed in the flame behind her.

Blaze felt her heart leap within her. *Pleased.* The Archmage had actually said that to her. A rush of emotion flooded her. She hadn't realized how badly she'd wanted someone from the Order to say that.

The Archmage's arm swirled in the air, until something long and slender formed within the flames: the outline of a staff. The Archmage's flaming form extended its arm until the fire staff hovered a mere foot from Blaze's face. The flame pulled back. In its place was a very real, wooden Ember Mage staff.

"We see that you have harnessed the power you had failed to control. We hoped for this," said the Archmage. "Take the staff. It is yours. By it, we restore you to the Order of Ember and grant you full rights as an Ember Mage."

Blaze caught her breath. This . . . this was everything she had not dared to hope for. She reached for the staff.

Then a thought struck her, and her fingers paused in the air. "But . . . why now?" she stammered.

The Archmage looked to Princess Sapphire's prone form on the floor. "You have the princess. Escape this war with her, and you will complete your mission. Some of us never doubted you," she said.

At that, Blaze burned a little. "Some of you?" she asked.

The Archmage's eyes darted back to the council

behind her. She hissed in a whisper. "Some of us feared your power. Some of us feared it might even eclipse their own and threaten the very council seats on which they sat."

"Others saw your potential," she said, holding Blaze's gaze. So she was part of the latter group.

Blaze swallowed. Now they saw. Now they believed.

"Blaze of Midway, you have always had the ever-burning flame inside you. That we have known from the beginning. Reckless, yes. Hot-tempered, undoubtedly, even for an Ember Mage. But we see you have learned to harness your anger."

Blaze took hold of the staff. It was warm to the touch. She gripped it with both hands, and heat flowed from it into her, and then back into the staff, generating a growing cycle of fire. Oh how badly she'd wanted this. She'd almost forgotten how good it felt.

"You must return the princess to Crystalia Castle," said the Archmage. "In doing so, you will bring honor to our Order."

The flame from the stove pulsed white, then curled into a glowing sphere of light. It was another portal, just like the one back in Crystalia Castle.

"Return the princess and join us, this time with a place in our council," said the Archmage.

Blaze's throat grew dry. It was so simple now. Step through the portal. Save Princess Sapphire. Complete the mission King Jasper had given her.

Rejoin the Ember Mages.

She lowered the staff in her hands. Then why did she hesitate? This *was* her purpose. But hadn't Dreck spoken of the tapestry that binds all things? The threads that tied them to the Goddess?

Dreck. Of all the foolish notions to pop into her head—Dreck was her friend.

She couldn't believe she was admitting that to herself. That ridiculous Crook-Eye monk who had saved her time and again. In the hot springs. From the village of Hetsa. Who had patiently put up with her anger. Her enemy. But also, more than anything, her friend.

Princess Sapphire needed her. But so did Dreck. So did Foruk's Falls for that matter. So did all of the Frostbyte Reach. The way of the Goddess was not saving one thread but pulling them all together. Hadn't he taught her that?

Now she was ready to listen.

Blaze pushed the staff back into the fire. The flames engulfed it slowly, and it hovered there, locked in place.

"What?" asked the Archmage. Her brows narrowed.

"I . . . can't," whispered Blaze.

"You cannot what?" said the Archmage, her voice tense.

Blaze pushed the staff again, and it was sucked into the flames until it was just out of reach. It burned to ash and disappeared from her view.

The Kings Summons

"It's not just about Princess Sapphire anymore. There are people who need me," said Blaze. There were soldiers trapped outside. If she left now with the princess, she would never have a chance to rescue Dreck, or stop the dark jotnar. And even despite the odds, her decision felt right. "I'm sure you understand."

The Archmage burned with fury, exploding with an angry light. Blaze stumbled backward, surprised by the show of power. "You *fool.*" The Archmage hissed. "They always doubted you—the girl with the scarlet eyes." She swept her hands back to indicate the council behind her. "I did not. You were broken. I said you could return. It is time for you to channel your anger. To concentrate your power! Do not fail me! Join me! Together we can tear down my rivals! Stand at my right hand!"

The fire curled and flashed an angry red. The council members huddled behind the Archmage, whispering amongst themselves. Blaze felt anger burning within her.

"We have only a few moments," said the Archmage. The spell was burning through the coal quickly. "A fire vision cannot last."

"No!" Blaze snapped, her eyebrows sparking with fury. The force of her rage seemed to push on the Archmage, who shrunk at Blaze's wrath. "*This* is what you worry about? Power? Control? Outsmarting your allies? No! There is more to save here than just the princess. The entire realm is at risk. We have to stop Cernonos. He has my friend."

"Madness!" cried the mages of the council, their disembodied voices filling the carriage.

That was the way of the Goddess, helping each other. Never giving up. Even if it meant risking the Prophecy. It wasn't about building anger and hatred for the enemy, much less anger and hatred for each other. Hadn't Princess Sapphire let the Crook-Eye Orcs go? And they had turned.

The flames flickered before her. The spell was beginning to unravel.

"End this madness, Blaze. Embrace your ambition. Step through the portal!" cried the Archmage.

Blaze forced her balled fists to open. "I don't know what I am," she said. "But I'm not just an Ember Mage. There's something else. I felt it hours ago—and it wasn't rage. It wasn't anger, but the spark was there."

"Don't do this!" The Archmage's voice spoke as if strained by the load of the spell. "Stay where you are. Rejoin the Order. Save the prin—"

Blaze kicked the grate shut and plunged the carriage into darkness.

She stood for a moment, alone in the blackness, devoid of feeling. Her rage was gone. She was empty, but that was good. It gave room for something new. She would need time to process all this.

"Ungh." Princess Sapphire moaned on the floor at Blaze's feet.

The Kings Summons

"Princess!" cried Blaze. She bent down to help.

Princess Sapphire waved her away.

"When did you wake up?" asked Blaze.

Princess Sapphire shook her head. "I'm not sure I have yet."

"Need some ice for your head? We've got plenty," said Blaze.

"Not funny."

The two burst into laughter.

"What . . . what happened?" groaned Princess Sapphire.

"Cernonos tossed us. I hit the snow. You hit a stone pillar."

"So that's why I feel like a smith has been using my head for an anvil. Did we . . . win?"

Blaze shook her head. "The dark jotnar . . . there was no way to stop it."

Princess Sapphire cursed. "We have to find a way."

"First we have to find a way out of here. It's a long walk back to Foruk's Falls."

"And the rest of our army?"

Blaze pointed upward. "Still up at the spawning point, frozen in solid ice."

"We have to find a way to free them," said Princess Sapphire.

There was a horrific clang of metal. It echoed down the tunnel and into the gap. It rang again, twice, then three times. Each time it sounded like a hammer hitting a gong.

Then a bearded head stuck itself into the window upside-down. "Hullo. Free who?" said the head. It was Tort, hanging upside down from the carriage's roof.

Blaze was so glad to see him, she almost hugged him. "But how did you get down here?"

"Used the stairs," said Tort. He made his fingers walk down the palm of his left hand, as if it were just that easy. "Well, after we broke free of the ice and then melted the orcs, that is. That little explosion made the ice brittle enough to break."

Princess Sapphire sat up. "What happened to Cernonos's army?"

Bort's head appeared in the window on the other side of the carriage. "They left in a real hurry," said Bort. "Probably headed straight to Foruk's Falls now that they're recharged. They didn't even take the time to finish us off. Took the dark jotnar with 'em too."

At least they were safe. Blaze let out a sigh.

"That means Cernonos and his men will capture the evacuated city and celebrate their victory tonight," said Princess Sapphire. She stood up carefully, testing her weight on her limbs. "We need a new plan."

The metal gong sounded again in their ears.

"What is all that racket?" asked Princess Sapphire.

"Oh, that!" said Tort, grinning so wide his beard parted, "That's the sound of our new ticket out of here.

The Kings Summons

Don't worry, we have got an incredibly great idea."

Chapter 19

The Core of Crystalia

Blaze lay atop the carriage, holding on for dear life as it sped down the track, the wind whistling in her hair. She really hoped the tunnel didn't have any unexpected stalactites waiting to decapitate her. She needed her head. She ventured a question. "Did anybody think about brakes?"

A couple of the dwarves had figured out how to decouple the last carriage from the rest of the train and detach the gears that meshed with the autowinders on the sides of the track. What was left was a free-wheeling, jam-packed, out of control train carriage speeding down the sloped tunnel toward Foruk's Falls.

Why did that worry Blaze?

The nominated dwarf coachman shrugged. "Princess wanted us to get to Foruk's Falls. Didn't say anything about stopping."

"Are you serious?" Blaze asked.

"Figured she had something in mind. Wouldn't she say something if she didn't?" said the dwarf coachman.

The dwarves and orcs hanging from every available handle, support, and foot runner on the carriage shored up their grips. It was amazing how many you could squeeze onto a carriage when you had to.

Bort poked his head up from the rear platform of the carriage. "Don't worry, I've got this!" he said, holding up a metal rod with a hook and spike on one end.

"That's a poker, Bort," said Blaze.

Bort nodded. "Aye. See, I'll just jam it down here on the track behind us, and we'll drag it on the ties until we slow down."

Blaze had been right to worry. She really needed to trust her hunches more. "Is that all you've got?" she asked.

"I've got a shovel!" cried another dwarf. He waved a shovel in the air. Maybe that would help a little.

"And he's got a sandwich," said Bort, pointing to Tort, who was just about to shove a two-foot-long sub sandwich into his mouth. He gave a sheepish grin.

"But it's only to be used in case of emergency," said Bort.

From inside the coach where Princess Sapphire and the dwarf princes were ostensibly talking strategy, a gruff voice bellowed, "Why aren't we going any faster?"

"Shimmies like a wheel is bent," said the coachman. "That tends to slow us down a bit."

Blaze gritted her teeth as the carriage descended a steep stretch in the dark tunnel. "That's a blessing from the Goddess," she said.

The Thunder Twins grumbled. Apparently they had other hopes.

"And now for the shortcut," said the coachman, a hint of excitement in his voice.

Blaze blinked. "What?"

"Parallel tunnels—they were built for one train to go up while the other was going down. There is a pressure switch that—"

"Yeah, but how short is this cut?" asked Blaze. Something on the tracks below made a loud pop. Blaze gave a scream of terror as the carriage tipped down in the darkness.

"That's more like it!" bellowed Tort.

The return trip had two possible outcomes: either they reached the end of the tunnel alive and managed to slow themselves with shovels and pokers, or the bent wheel

242

broke and they careened off the rails to a grisly fate.

The clattering of the carriage over the tracks grew louder and louder.

There was a bump and then suddenly silence.

"What was that?" asked Blaze.

"What was what?" said the nominated coachman.

They turned the corner and emerged into a large cavern filled with a crystal clear, underground, glowing blue lake—just like the pools Blaze had seen on the first leg of their journey, only many times larger. The glow seemed to come from deep down inside the waters, fading as it reached the surface, then shimmering across the cavern walls in a soft blue.

The track ran along the lake's edge, but that wasn't what troubled Blaze. It was more the fact that the track was a long way back, and the carriage was careening through the air, plummeting toward the middle of the lake.

The wheels had jumped the track.

Dwarves and orcs leapt from the falling carriage, some screaming and others giving great whoops of excitement.

The Thunder Twins bailed from either side, one attempting a cannon ball and the other going for a grand belly flop.

Blaze felt herself fly free from the carriage, her stomach leaping up into her throat as her arms pinwheeled before her face found the water with a smack.

She smashed through the water's surface, the cold

shocking her like a ton of bricks dropped on her lungs, forcing out every last degree of heat in her body with one magnificent blow. Her eyes flew open, and she looked up. In that instant, she saw the carriage sinking, a swarm of bubbles floating to the surface around it, and dwarves and orcs smashing into the water, one after another.

Blaze fought back panic. Her immediate instinct was to kick to the surface, to fight the cold, to find air. But first she needed to get control of herself.

She hesitated. The blue glow beneath her pulsed just like the gem on Princess Sapphire's sword had, as if it were calling her. It was giving off warmth in waves. It was majestic. And beautiful. A shining gem inviting her close.

Suddenly, she was calm again. Without thinking, Blaze dove downward, kicking toward the Princess-Sapphire-blue glow.

This was madness. She would run out of air. But the further she went, the warmer the water became, until it charged up her body once again, replenishing her, filling her up, and washing away her pains.

The essence of the Goddess. The spirit of the Goddess was strong here.

Blaze of Midway, weave yourself into the tapestry. The thought was as clear and precise as if a voice had said it to her.

How? thought Blaze.

Weave together. Forgive. Save Dreck. Win the day.

The Kings Summons

It wasn't a voice this time. She just *knew*. Dreck—the enemy would have taken him back to Foruk's Falls as a hostage. He needed her.

A burst of warmth and light hit Blaze. She arched her back and spread her arms, soaking it in, capturing it, absorbing it until it became part of her.

The Goddess was not gone. Blaze could feel it in her bones. A switch flipped inside her.

Reluctant to leave, she swam to the surface and broke through, gasping for air. It had all lasted less than a minute, but that was enough.

When she reached the shore, most of the dwarves and orcs were already there, shivering violently, teeth chattering loudly as they huddled together on the cold rocks.

The rest were still swimming ashore, dragging themselves out of the water with numb limbs while others tried to help.

They were a sorry looking lot, mangled and beaten by battle—and now this.

Even with as much bravado as they had just moments before, Bort and Tort's faces had turned dangerously blue, and the light had gone from their eyes. Icicles had already formed on a few of the dwarves' beards. They were cold, and if some something didn't warm them all soon in the subzero tunnel, they would freeze and die.

"Ember Mage . . ." said Bort in a weak whisper.

They needed her. Their lives depended on her power.

This was not an act of battle, but an act of kindness. Not an act of violence, but an act of love. In this moment, her fire had to be a gift.

Bort didn't even have to finish his sentence. Blaze summoned her fire.

But this time it was different. This time, instead of tapping into her anger to light the spark, she paused, and reached for something else that was close at hand, that *wanted* to be found: she tapped into the core of Crystalia. She felt herself as a thread in the tapestry of all things. She felt the connection to the Goddess. Heat flooded into her, deep inside her chest, just like it had in the depths of the lake.

Then she lit herself into a human torch. She coaxed the flame, up and out of her, curling it around her in a torus, then spinning it, recirculating the heat and moving the air like a desert wind.

The dwarves and orcs took two steps back, some of them shielding their eyes from the heat. Blaze kept the flame circulating, pushing the warmth outward.

At first the flame was red, but the longer she burned it, the deeper she drew from the essence of Crystalia she had just touched, the more the flame began to burn *white*.

And she did not lose strength as she burned it.

The dwarves and orcs began to stir, hopping in place and turning as the fire streaming over Blaze baked the cold out of them and turned it into a cloud of hissing steam.

The icicles on their beards melted away, and Bort's face turned a healthy pink again. Even the tips of the orcs' noses were red with the heat. As each dwarf or orc regained his composure, he stopped to stare at Blaze with mouth hung open.

"Your eyes," said Bort, his jaw agape.

Princess Sapphire took a step forward. She peered into Blaze's face, dumbfounded. "They're white," she said.

White. The world hadn't turned red this time when she'd summoned the flame. Something had changed. Something had grown inside her.

"In all my travels of Crystalia, I have never seen such a thing," whispered Princess Sapphire in awe, her deep blue eyes so wide, Blaze could see her reflection burning in them. She saw her own eyes, and they indeed were glowing *white.*

The princess raised her fingers, as if to reach out and touch Blaze, then hesitated as if she thought better of it.

So they had seen it too. Blaze had struck upon something wholly different. In doing this act for them, she'd taken some of the essence she'd felt in the depths of the lake. She'd weaved herself into the tapestry.

She let her flame slow, then flicker, then fade away. But the glow stayed in her heart.

"Hey, my trousers shrank!" cried a dwarf as he inspected his ankles.

"You look like a fat man in a pair of women's knickers!" bellowed the dwarf closest him.

Princess Sapphire stared at them both, as if she were reluctant for anyone to break the spell. Then she spoke. "At least you won't freeze solid again the moment we climb outside of the tunnel," she said.

She studied Blaze for another moment. It looked like there was something puzzling her. A slippery thought she was trying to grasp.

"Blaze . . ." she said, then never finished her sentence. Instead, she looked like she'd made up her mind about something. She found a stick and drew a map of Foruk's Falls in a patch of mud.

"We have only a few miles between us and the city. There are several access hatches we can climb out of before we reach the gates. Approaching the city undetected won't be a problem."

"But we need a new plan," said Bort.

Princess Sapphire stabbed the mud several times. "Here are the secret entrances to the city. The Torch Road and Everlight Express platforms are sure to be guarded heavily now, but there are still the cracks between the mountain and wall, and the old siege tunnel."

Tort looked over her shoulder. He made a new mark in the mud. "And the east gate is too small to guard with a large fighting force," he said. "No one would think of that as the attack point for a major onslaught."

"Then we'll focus our main attack there and draw the Rimefrost Orcs' attention away from the second and third squads who will have snuck in through the secret entrances," said the princess.

She turned to the dwarf archers. "I want a hail of arrows coming at them from all sides before we break through that gate."

They nodded and saluted in response. Dwarves were never much for words.

"What about the jotnar?" asked Tort. It seemed to be the question on everyone's mind.

Princess Sapphire turned to look at Blaze. Blaze met her eyes. They seemed to say, "Your turn." The princess didn't know. She needed a plan.

"How many metal shields do we have left?" asked Blaze.

Bort looked around them. "That aren't at the bottom of the lake?" he asked. "Maybe a dozen or so."

"And gloves?" asked Blaze. All the dwarves held up thick leather gloves. The orcs' knuckles were bare.

"Good. Form up in squads, a half dozen or so men to each shield bearer. Stick close to each other," said Blaze. A plan was starting to form in her head. She had no idea if it would work, but it was better than no plan at all.

Princess Sapphire looked over Blaze appraisingly. She gave the slightest nod as if to approve. "Everyone stays out of sight for as long as possible. Do not engage the dark jotnar until absolutely necessary. Follow Blaze's lead. Any arguments to the contrary?"

"But what about the dark jotnar?!" Tort asked again. He stomped his feet. It was very unlike him. "Are we forgetting that just hours ago, it defeated us hands down? We nearly lost our entire little army. Metal shields and secret entrances aside, we're no match for it."

Bort put a hand on his brother's shoulder. Nearly freezing to death had seemed to take some bite out of both of the Thunder Twins. The orcs nodded in agreement.

Princess Sapphire dropped her stick. "We have something new now that no one has ever had before," she said. They all looked at her, orc and dwarf alike, as if waiting for her very next word.

Princess Sapphire looked at Blaze. "We have the first White Ember Mage."

Chapter 20

A Battle of Fire and Ice

Blaze waited silently, hidden in the trees outside Foruk's Falls with her squad, her eyes focused on the city's gate. Her chest burned with fire.

Princess Sapphire had taken one squad with her toward the crack at the base of the mountain. Bort and Tort had led the other into the siege tunnel.

A familiar raven fluttered down from the sky and landed on Blaze's shoulder. "Hello Rav," she said. She ruffled his head feathers. He would know where they were keeping Dreck. "We'll help him, Rav. I promise," she said. She found that she meant it.

Get into the city. Find Dreck. Stop the dark jotnar. Defeat Cernonos.

The dwarves' and Crook-Eye Orcs' slow, methodical breathing sent puffs of steam into the frigid air.

A hail of arrows shot skyward from inside the city. A moment later, and a second hail flew from the opposite direction near the place where the mountain met the city wall. The dwarf archers had begun the attack. The city erupted in the shouts and clangs of battle.

"Now!" cried Blaze. She charged forward, her hands glowing fire, the squad of dwarves and Crook-Eye Orcs trailing behind her. This time, just like back in the tunnel, the scene did not turn red. It was white. As she ran, she looked down at her burning hands. The red flame was tipped in a silver-white glow.

She shot out two columns of flame, blasting the Rimefrost Orc guards that stood atop the tiny wooden gate and knocking them back off the wall.

She shot a second concussive fireball straight at the wooden gate. It was only wide enough for a single dwarf to pass through at a time, but the wood was thick and studded with metal spikes.

It broke easily anyway, splintering into tiny shards as soon as her fireball hit it.

Blaze shot through the narrow opening. "Fire Wave!"

she said, blasting out a wave of protective red and silver fire as soon as she cleared the gate.

The pressure from the Fire Wave knocked over several Rimefrost Orcs who were advancing on the gate.

On the other side of the wall was the city park and behind that, the magnificent, enormous, blue icicle that was the frozen waterfall. At its base was a large open area. That was where the jotnar would be.

And the danger.

Several orc encampments with bonfires littered the city park. There must have been at least a hundred Rimefrost Orcs just in the park, with gnolls and kobolds mixed in between.

Rav flew ahead, dodging and weaving until he landed on the barred windowsill of a distant tower on the other side of the river. He turned and cawed at Blaze.

Dreck. *That's where they're holding Dreck.*

Blaze ran across the square, blasting Rimefrost Orcs as she went. Behind her, the sounds of battle raged as sword clanged against ax, and dwarves, orcs, gnolls, and kobolds clashed.

She blasted one kobold, then a gnoll, then another. Each successive fireball was more silvery-white than the last as it shot from her palms, until she rolled, unleashing a Fire Wave of pure white flame at a line of attacking Rimefrost Orcs.

Blaze shed her white fur coat—it was too easy to spot

against the backdrop of painted stone houses behind her. Plus, she needed to be free, to move without restriction. She was not cold, not now.

She surged forward, all the while twisting and turning, fireballs blasting into Rimefrost Orcs, knocking them out of the battle. She was a whirlwind of motion and flame, the strange, new white fire filling her core and clearing her vision.

Blaze would never have been able to concentrate on so many enemies at once with red fire. Too much of that came from raw anger. But the white fire cleared her head and opened her senses until she was able to feel the whole scene before her and around her: the position of each orc, the swing of each ax, the rhythm of the battle.

She knocked back wave after wave of advancing Rimefrost Orcs, dispatching them with grace and precision.

Dreck. Must get Dreck.

She charged the tower.

Forty paces away. Then Thirty. Then twenty.

The ground shook beneath her. Boom. Boom. Two dull impacts, one tremor after another, then a third. Footsteps.

A shadow passed over the city park and stretched to the frozen river beneath the falls. For a moment, the battle seemed to stop.

Blaze looked up mid-stride. The ice-blue form of the dark jotnar towered above her, skin laced with red runes,

Iron Collar clamped about its neck, eyes glowing ember.

She changed direction, pivoting off her right foot and darting hard left. She needed to be ready.

Her army behind her had broken into several squads, each made up of a shield-bearing dwarf, a few dwarf spearmen, and some orcs with battle axes. The other squads with the archers would be out in front, somewhere to her right and left, hidden from view.

"Fire Cloud!" she said, casting three fireballs up at the jotnar's head, each one more for show than actual damage. She just needed to distract it. She needed to buy them a little time.

"Form up!" cried the nearest shield-bearing dwarf.

The dark jotnar wound its arm back like it was about to throw, then hurled a blast of freezing ice particles at Blaze. She dodged, and the dark jotnar hurled another ice blast, this time aimed at the squad right behind her. Blaze felt the sting of stray ice crystals on her face and watched as the blast froze a swath of the city solid. Good thing she wasn't in the center of the concentrated blast. That one would have been deadly.

But their little army had been expecting exactly that. As soon as the dark jotnar had hurled its first blast of ice, the squads each formed into a tight single file line with the shield-bearing dwarf in front.

Blaze summoned the fire from the core of Crystalia, drawing it deep from the Goddess's essence. She channeled her heat—without flame—into the first dwarf's metal shield. It was harder at this distance, but she did it, forcing the metal to suck in the heat like a magnet.

The shield superheated, glowing orange as the pocket of air closest to it shimmered.

The next blast from the jotnar slammed into the dwarf's shield. But the dwarf was ready with his heels dug in. The superheated metal shield melted the core of the ice column and the pocket of hot air split the blast to either side of the dwarf like a boulder in a river.

The edges of the ice blast—now warmed by the shield— frosted over the dwarves' and orcs' arms harmlessly, so that they looked like they'd been dusted with a light snow.

"Huzzah!" cried the dwarves. The Crook-Eye Orcs grunted in triumph. They had survived an attack.

Fortunately, Blaze had instructed each shield-bearing dwarf to wrap their gloved hands in thick leather hides.

And her plan was working. Blaze forced heat into the other squads' shields. Better to be prepared.

Then she charged forward, dodging ice blast after ice blast from the jotnar.

The dwarves and Crook-Eye Orcs broke each one with their superheated shields, their squads taking cover safely behind.

By now, Bort's and Tort's squads had converged with their dwarf archers into the city square. Axes out, their soldiers joined the fray.

256

The Kings Summons

An orc raised a short sword, winding up to bring it down on Bort's head. "Fire Shot!" Blaze shot it with a column of flame, knocking him sideways.

She looked up to see Dreck gripping the bars in the window of the tower across the river where Rav had landed. So he *was* there. She felt relief wash over her.

The jotnar roared, the red runes pulsing on its skin, and brought its foot smashing down mere inches from Blaze's back.

She rolled and dodged. *Can't let myself get distracted,* she thought, bringing her mind back from the breadth of the battle and focusing on the moment.

She thrust both fists upward, shooting a concentrated white fire blast into the jotnar's chest.

The blast dug in, carving a bright red scar across its blue skin. It roared, releasing a soundwave that shook the city walls and trees.

The wave knocked Blaze to her knees, and she stumbled, then leapt to her feet, still trembling from the sound.

The dark jotnar stretched its arms out to either side and shot ice from its hands until two huge icicles formed on each arm. They were as enormous as jagged mountain peaks. The jotnar bent low and swung its left arm-spike outward like a claw, sweeping across the battlefield and cutting a swath through dwarf, kobold, gnoll, and Rimefrost and Crook-Eye Orc alike.

Adam Glendon Sidwell and Zachary James

Soldiers on either side littered the battlefield, crying out in pain.

Horrified, Blaze dove between the jotnar's feet and came out on the other side behind it. What had she done? Those were her dwarves. Those were her Crook-Eye Orcs. She hadn't meant any harm to come to them.

But there was nothing she could do for them at that moment. She had to focus. *Must save Dreck.* That *was* something she could do.

She leapt out over the river, blasting the ground behind her with a column of flame. The fire boosted her up and over the frozen water, many times as high as she could normally jump. She landed on the opposite bank as the dark jotnar turned.

Good. She'd distracted it.

It locked its eyes on her and roared again. It swung its arm-spike down at her, narrowly missing her head and smashing into the tower where Dreck was prisoner.

"Blaze!" Dreck cried from the window as the tower's foundation shattered. The tower wobbled dangerously.

Blaze wasted no time. She pressed both palms into the ground, then, with a blast of white fire, shot herself straight up into the air like a rock from a catapult. She felt her stomach lurch, then cut off the flame and slowed, hanging in midair for a split second in front of Dreck's window.

She caught the sides of the sill with both hands and

258

landed nimbly on the ledge. Then, igniting the side of her hand in glowing plasma, Blaze sliced through the iron bars.

Dreck smiled his horrible smile. "I knew you would come."

Blaze smiled back, on the verge of tears. "I knew you would be here."

"Blaze funny," Dreck said.

"We have to get out of here," Blaze said. She grabbed Dreck's hand, but it didn't budge. He held her firm in his grip.

What?

Was it a trick?

She looked into his eyes and saw her glowing white eyes, much like she had in Princess Sapphire's. Never in history had an Ember Mage channeled white fire.

White was beyond the heat of the Crystalia's core—it was the fire of the stars.

The light of the Goddess.

This was what Dreck had taught her to do. He could not be her enemy. He never was.

Blaze stopped struggling.

Dreck reached into his robe and drew out his hand. His fist opened slowly.

The setting sun sent dazzling sparkles off a glittering, heart-shaped object.

"The locket!" cried Blaze. She never thought she would

see King Jasper's gift again.

Dreck held it out and lifted it over Blaze's neck.

"But how—when?" Blaze asked. Dreck had left her at the hot springs. He had left her alone and then come back. It made sense. "You got my locket back from the goblins, didn't you?"

Dreck nodded.

"Blaze treat Dreck like enemy. Dreck do like princess," Dreck said. "Treat Blaze like friend."

"And we are," Blaze said. She confessed it. She would do anything for Dreck. She grasped both of his shoulders.

Unbidden, the locket opened just a crack. It shone with a dazzling white light, begging Blaze to open it.

Wait, she thought. *Not yet.*

The tower wobbled dangerously once more. *Time to act.* With a surge of strength powered by the fire within, she pulled Dreck from the window and leapt downward. She blasted a column of white flame from one palm and slowed their descent before she hit the ground. Dreck tumbled away into the snow and Blaze skidded nimbly, still on her feet.

The tower collapsed, smashing into the ground in a billow of dust and rubble behind them.

"Come on, Dreck. We're going to free the jotnar," said Blaze. Dreck nodded, leaping to his feet.

The sounds of battle across the river drew Blaze's attention back to the fray. Where was Princess Sapphire?

The Kings Summons

Of course. She would strike at the crux. She would go after Cernonos.

Blaze scanned the battlefield. Now that the tower was gone Blaze could see them clearly at the foot of the enormous frozen falls. There she was: Princess Sapphire locked in combat with Cernonos.

The princess's sword slashed like a moving lightning bolt, driving Cernonos backward, giving him no chance to conjure fire or snare her in his vine-like fingers.

The jotnar turned its head, drawn by Blaze's gaze toward the master who had given it the collar. It raised its arm.

"Princess Sapphire, look out!" Blaze cried.

The dark jotnar hurled its right arm-spike free from its hand, straight at the princess like an enormous javelin.

Princess Sapphire leapt forward with impossible speed, her blue-tinged armor blurring as she rolled away.

The giant icicle spear buried itself deep in the base of frozen Foruk's Falls, cracking the ice.

Princess Sapphire flipped to her feet, only to dodge a swipe from Cernonos's horns. The jotnar hurled its remaining arm-spike at her, forcing her to dodge yet again.

The edge of the icicle scraped the back of her armor, hurling her forward and behind a wall of ice where she was cut off from Blaze's view. The princess was tiring. She couldn't face both enemies alone. Blaze had to do something fast.

"Dreck, go!" Blaze called. Motioning up toward the dark jotnar.

They had to get to the Iron Collar.

"Dreck! Go now," cried Blaze. The jotnar lifted its foot to turn and Dreck raced forward.

But the jotnar was quicker than it looked. It shot a blast of ice toward Dreck, freezing him in place where he stood.

A spear whipped past Blaze, hissing as it passed her ear. She turned to see a line of gnolls advancing on her, with two hulking Rimefrost Orcs not far behind them. They drew back their spears. They had caught up to her.

Stupid, Blaze. That lapse of concentration had almost cost her. She'd have to pay better attention to the entire battlefield again. For the first time since breaking through the gate, the thrill of battle broke, and fear took hold of Blaze's heart. She couldn't fight them all. There were just too many. Cernonos. The dark jotnar. An army of enemies. She couldn't save the princess.

The jotnar turned and trudged toward Dreck's frozen body. One step would be enough to smash him to bits.

Then she would be alone. She could not succeed alone. Then she reached into the space between all of them: Dreck, the dwarves, the Crook-Eye Orcs. It was filled with the essence of the Goddess. The light of the stars.

The secret magic.

The Kings Summons

Loyalty. Sacrifice. Hope. Love.

A burst of flame filled her. The locket sprang open and a flash of white fire wrapped Blaze in a tornado of light and heat. The metal locket unfolded, unlocking and telescoping out across her chest like an impossible puzzle, until it was twice, then three, then ten times its mass. It covered her chest in a series of interlocking red and silvery-white plates, like the scales of a dragon, then grew out across her arms and legs, until finally, gauntlets covered both hands. A helmet with flame-wings flipped over her head and locked itself into place, a visor clamping down to protect her eyes.

Blaze looked down in awe at the metal alloy covering her body. It shimmered red and silvery-white and glowed with power and strength. This felt *good*.

She *was* the White Ember Mage.

She turned as a hail of spears, hatchets, and daggers from the gnolls at her back flew straight at her. There were too many to dodge. They were going to strike her heart.

But before they could reach her, a cloud of glowing white fire surrounding her armor incinerated the weapons. They fell to the ground as white ash.

This felt *really good*.

Blaze pivoted, then raced forward toward Dreck as the entire enemy army turned their firepower on her—the armored White Ember Mage.

Another hail of spears and daggers flew at her. Her

armor pulsed unbidden, releasing a wave of white fire and melting the weapons in midair. She spun, even as she ran toward Dreck, her momentum carrying her forward, while she threw her arms back. The scaled plates on her forearms snapped open, and jets of silver-white flame shot from beneath them, knocking the entire wave of enemy orcs and gnolls off their feet.

By all of Crystalia, how had she not used this armor before? This was very, very cool.

But the dark jotnar had reached its quarry. It lifted its foot over Dreck and brought it smashing down.

"NO!" Blaze shouted. It came out as more of a command than a cry of desperation, and she surged forward, her armor carrying her at the speed of flame.

In a blur, she reached Dreck, raised both gauntlets high and *caught* the foot of the jotnar at the arch.

Impossible, yet there she was, holding up the foot of the massive dark jotnar, one thousand times her weight. It pressed her into the ground, the mass of a mountain bearing down on her. She struggled, each limb and joint straining against the incredible force. The ball of the foot pressed into Dreck's frozen skull. If it went much further, it would crush him.

No. Dreck is my friend.

Blaze summoned all her strength and the armor began to pulse silver-white. Waves of red flashed out across its surface.

The Kings Summons

She heaved the foot backward and the jotnar stumbled.

She had a mere moment to act. Blaze leapt, the strength of her fire-armor carrying her high into the air. She landed on the jotnar's chest with both feet, smashing it backward. It fell, and as it fell, it shot ribbons of ice like roots into the ground for support.

They weren't enough. Blaze's impact broke the ice supports, and the dark jotnar crashed against the riverbank, shattering the river ice.

In two bounding steps, she reached the Iron Collar and took hold of it with both hands. The red rune lines writhed and pulsed like angry worms. The collar had mocked her fire. Now she would give it everything she had.

She flooded the metal with heat. Slowly, the cold iron took on a white glow, then yellow, then orange.

The dark jotnar roared, convulsing in pain. It twisted, nearly throwing Blaze from its chest. She held on as tightly as she could, whipping around violently as the jotnar writhed.

The red runes began to flash more quickly now. The more heat Blaze poured in, the faster they pulsed.

The Iron Collar was melting!

Blaze screamed as she tried to pull the collar apart. The metal stretched like molten glass.

White fire poured out of her gauntlets, encasing the iron in a glowing white field of flame.

With a crack, Blaze snapped the Iron Collar in two. The glowing red runes winked out. She flung the two softened half-circles of metal away from the jotnar's neck, into the freezing river.

Then she flipped backward off the jotnar's chest and landed on her feet on the riverbank. The jotnar closed its eyes and fell back onto the ground, as if it were asleep. It struck with such force, she had to brace herself where she stood.

She had done it. The jotnar was free.

The lump of ice surrounding Dreck cracked and broke. Blaze had not realized how close she'd landed to him. The heat from her armor was melting the ice. "Dreck?" she said, desperation in her voice.

She turned to free him, but his arm smashed through the ice before she could take a step. In another instant, he'd broken his torso and arms free.

Sopping wet and shivering, Dreck spread his arms. "Hug?" he said.

Blaze's armor flared. "Certainly. But not yet," said Blaze. She couldn't risk burning him. She'd save a big hug for him after this was all through.

Blaze looked toward the falls, where Princess Sapphire now faced Cernonos alone.

His arms had become mighty black swords. They swept through the ice, slashing with such force at Princess Sapphire that they cut huge chunks of the falls away.

266

The Kings Summons

Princess Sapphire dodged and parried, her sword shining blue as she swung it in ever tightening arcs.

Blaze rushed forward with an armor-powered sprint. *She can't outfight him*, Blaze realized. She readied a final blast.

Cernonos swung down with both black sword-arms.

For a moment Princess Sapphire flickered, and Blaze thought she saw several different versions of the princess reflect across facets of the frozen falls. In an instant the reflection was gone, and Princess Sapphire stood, cornered in a semicircle of a dozen great icicles.

Cernonos struck, stabbing his black sword-arms into the place where Princess Sapphire stood.

"Princess Sapphire!" Blaze cried. Her heart filled with dread. Had she really just seen that? Had the princess really just—Blaze couldn't finish the thought.

Her armor surged forward, closing the last few yards to the falls.

She let out an enormous white blast of heat, a column of flame larger in diameter than she was tall, like an enormous tunnel of fire. It struck the base of the frozen falls, cutting right through the ice, emptying out all the flame and heat ever stored inside her. Blazed forced herself into the flame, as if she was the fire and the fire was her.

The ice hissed, releasing a billowing cloud of steam so thick, Cernonos disappeared from view.

The falls trembled, then shook as its foundation

cracked and gave way. Then, slowly, as if in painful slow motion, the huge frozen column of ice fell, crashing down on the place where Cernonos stood.

The impact blew the steam away in a gust of pressurized air. Sheets of river ice surged outward in waves.

The demon Cernonos was buried in a tomb of ice.

And on one of the flat chunks of ice, riding it in a poised crouch as it surged forward, was Princess Sapphire, her armor tinged in blue, and her blue hair flowing out behind her.

She skidded to a stop only two steps away from Blaze and dismounted. "Thank you very much for your flame, dear White Ember Mage," she said, bowing to Blaze. "It could not have come at a better time." Then Princess Sapphire pinched her own chin, as if a thought had struck her. "Unless of course, you'd come several minutes earlier."

Blaze smirked, then chuckled. "You're quite welcome then, Princess." Then she remembered what she saw. "But Cernonos struck you with his blades. How are you here?"

"When there's a fight you can't win, you change the fight," said Princess Sapphire. She held an empty, round potion bottle in one hand. "I was all out of concealment potion of course, but not out of reflecting potion." She tossed the glass bottle over her shoulder. It shattered when it hit the ground. "That wasn't me. It was just a reflection of me," she said.

So that's what Blaze had seen flicker in the ice. Princess

The Kings Summons

Sapphire never ceased to amaze.

The princess looked down at Blaze's armor. "New suit? I *like* it."

Blaze glanced down. The shimmer of flame across the metal scales had begun to fade, probably drained by her last great burst of fire.

Still, her suit *was* impressive. Blaze pressed the metal locket on her chest and the armor began to click and fold into itself, like a hundred dominos, until the entire suit had retracted into a single heart-shaped locket again.

"Keep that," said Princess Sapphire, pointing to the locket. "It might come in handy someday."

She didn't have to tell Blaze twice.

The fallen ice which had once been Foruk's Falls flashed red, then gave way to blackness.

The demon Cernonos was gone.

In the city park, the Rimefrost Orcs, gnolls, and kobolds were beating a hasty retreat as the dwarves and Crook-Eye Orcs chased the last of them out of the city.

Behind Blaze, the jotnar, red lines now gone from its skin, sighed softly in its sleep.

Dreck wrapped his arms around Blaze from behind in a giant big-brother bear hug. "Hug now!" he said. Blaze didn't object. She wriggled around, then hugged him right back. It felt good.

"We won," said Princess Sapphire. She flashed a grin.

"I couldn't have done it alone," Blaze said.

"Same goes for me," said the princess, with a smile. "But don't you dare tell my father I said that."

Dreck and Blaze laughed. Suddenly, Blaze felt the tension of battle break. They *had* won. They had defeated Cernonos. And here they were. Alive.

"Of course, there will be the Freyr to deal with," said Princess Sapphire.

Blaze looked at her. She wasn't sure what she meant by that.

"You've destroyed his waterfall," said Princess Sapphire. "They'll have to rename the town."

"To Foruk Fell?" asked Dreck.

Blaze groaned. Dreck gave a roar of a laugh, and they turned toward the city gates. It was time to recall the exiles of Foruk's Falls.

It was time to celebrate.

Chapter 21

Return

"Sire, the portal—it's opening on its own!"

King Jasper III raced down the hall of the castle after his wizened master magician.

A swirl of white light filled the Crystal Chamber behind the king's war room and formed into a small tornado of flickering energy.

"Who is it?" King Jasper asked.

"I'm not sure," said the magician. "It is still too faint to tell."

"Reach out to it," commanded the king. "Summon your magic."

The magician lifted a staff and whispered a spell, speaking to the song of the Goddess that rang through the crystals of the room. In response, the light doubled, tripled in size.

"It's the Reach!" the king cried. He could see the frozen, jagged horizon inside the portal. His heart nearly exploded. He wanted to hope, but he didn't dare. Not yet. "It's the Reach! I can see the peaks."

Flecks of snow brushed the king's face as the room swirled with a gust of cold air.

"Keep it open!" King Jasper called.

"I . . . can't," said the magician, struggling to keep his staff aloft. "It's too far away."

The king could not let it close. There was too much at stake. He would not lose her again. He lifted his scepter and slammed it down on the ground, releasing a flash of pure energy.

His body, sapped of strength, collapsed. They were so close. *My daughter. Please let it be my daughter.* He propped himself up on one knee.

The portal finally swelled as tall as a human.

Within the tornado of light, a form grew, coalescing into a shining blue silhouette. Then the white light was gone, and in its place stood Princess Sapphire's sparkling armor.

The Kings Summons

The master magician fell to one knee.

"You are found!" King Jasper cried. "You are found! My daughter, Princess Sapphire has returned!"

Princess Sapphire stepped out of the place where the white portal had been. King Jasper climbed to his feet and collapsed onto his daughter, wrapping his arms around her shoulders, feeling the chill of her armor as it bit against his cheek.

She removed her helmet and kissed his cheek.

"Hello, King Worrywart," Princess Sapphire said.

King Jasper looked into her eyes. "My daughter. Tell me, is there hope for the Frostbyte Reach?"

Princess Sapphire just smiled.

King Jasper III grinned through his gushing tears of joy. "How . . . how did you get here?"

"A little luck, and lot of fire."

The bells of Castletown rang through the halls of the citadel and echoed in the streets of the city. Far out in the Fae Wood, the sensitive ears of the elves turned toward the center of the realm.

From the base of the Frostbyte peaks, not far away from where the city of Midway once stood, spring grass spread out across the valley like a sea of green. In its center, a newly constructed tower rose toward the heavens. A lone Ember Mage stood on the parapets, overlooking her domain.

The tower's tiled roof was red. Its walls were built of glistening alabaster and ivory, with silvery-white metal spires.

Her orc friend stood next to her. They had built it, together—orc and human.

Blaze looked over the waves of grain in the fallow fields on the borders of a derelict village.

Midway.

Inside her mind, Blaze could still hear the words Dreck had spoken so often. "Open your heart. See with your heart."

She pointed to a clearing near Midway's edge. "This is where I'll start my school," she said. She pointed to a space across the street where Crook-Eye Orcs were already dragging great logs into the village. "And this is where the orphanage will be."

Dreck smiled his horrible grin. "A town big enough for me to wander in," he said.

Reaching within herself, Blaze felt for the thing that connected them all. The essence that bound them together.

She spun in a circle and released a burst of white fire.

Rising into the air, she spun faster and faster until at last she lifted her arms and let fly a burst of light so great it was seen from Crystalia Castle's battlements.

The White Ember Mage's domain was now Crystalia Castle's rear guard—a pinnacle of hope.

274

The Kings Summons

The dwarves of the Reach now had a chance to stand up to their enemies. And so could all the creatures of Crystalia. They would fight the Dark Consul. They *could* hold back the darkness.

Princess Sapphire, princess of prophecy, had been found.

Read all the books in the Super Dungeon Series!
Coming soon, wherever books are sold.
To find out more, visit

https://www.futurehousepublishing.com/super-dungeon-series/

Never miss a Future House release!

Sign up for the Future House Publishing email list:
www.futurehousepublishing.com/beta-readers-club

Connect with Future House Publishing

www.facebook.com/FutureHousePublishing

twitter.com/FutureHousePub

www.youtube.com/FutureHousePublishing

www.instagram.com/FutureHousePublishing

WANT TO KNOW MORE?

YOUR QUEST HAS JUST BEGUN.

Explore the adventure, tabletop
Gaming Experience, that started
it all.

www.ninjadivision.com

Acknowledgments

Of course I have to start by thanking Adam Glendon Sidwell, my coauthor, mentor, and friend. He took a chance on letting me help with this project, both in regards to drafting out the series, and in letting me help write this final manuscript. It was and is always a pleasure and an honor to collaborate with him.

Next, I want to thank Deke Stella, who let me play around in his world and forgave me when I got all the details wrong in my first couple of drafts, both in regards to my series pitch, and in subsequent drafts of this manuscript. I hope we get a chance to work together again in the future.

I also must thank Emma Hoggan, my favorite editor, and my good friend. She was instrumental in improving my initial drafts of the manuscript, and in improving upon my initial concepts and designs for the series as a whole. Without her improving my notes, concepts, and story beats, this book would have been much weaker overall.

A special word goes out to my wife Kirsta, who supported me in writing this book even when I took time away from her to do it.

Finally, I want to thank you, the reader, who spent time reading not only this book, but also these acknowledgements. I mean, who even does that? Someone pretty awesome is who.

Zachary James Strickland.

Adam Glendon Sidwell

In between books, Adam Glendon Sidwell uses the power of computers to make monsters, robots, and zombies come to life for blockbuster movies such as *Pirates of the Caribbean, King Kong, Pacific Rim, Transformers,* and *Tron.*

After spending countless hours in front of a keyboard meticulously adjusting tentacles, calibrating hydraulics, and brushing monkey fur, he is delighted at the prospect of modifying his creations with the flick of a few deftly placed adjectives. He once lived in New Zealand with the elves, so feels very qualified to write this fantasy series.

Adam also wrote every single word in the *Evertaster* series, the picture book *Fetch*, and the unfathomable *Chum.*

Connect with him at
facebook.com/AdamGlendonSidwell

Zachary James

Zachary James is the very creative pen name of Zachary James Strickland. By day, he's a mild-mannered mortgage specialist, but by night, he's a mild-mannered author.

Zachary graduated from Brigham Young University in 2017. He currently lives with his beautiful wife and trouble-making cocker spaniel in Salt Lake City, Utah.

Want Adam to come to your school?

Adam Glendon Sidwell has visited hundreds of schools across the country sharing his interactive assemblies and encouraging students to read and write. Adam uses visuals from his career as an animator for blockbuster Hollywood films such as *Tron, Pirates of the Caribbean,* and *Thor* to teach kids about writing structure, narrative, and theme. Adam's assembly is the perfect educational experience for your school.

For more information visit: http://www.futurehousepublishing.com/authors/ adamglendonsidwell/

Contact schools@futurehousepublishing.com to book Adam at your school.

CPSIA information can be obtained
at www.ICGtesting.com
Printed in the USA
FSHW022331110619
58970FS